A DIFFERENT DIAMOND

JODY STUDDARD

www.jstuddard.com

A Different Diamond

Cover Design: Jody Studdard
Cover Model: Amanda Tsujikawa

ISBN-10: 1489564934
ISBN-13: 978-1489564931

Softball Star
books by
Jody Studdard

A Different Diamond
Fastpitch Fever
Dog in the Dugout
Missfits Fastpitch
Silence in Center

Coming Soon!

Fastpitch U

Kiana Cruise
books by
Jody Studdard

Apocalypse
Multiplicity

For Amanda,
Lindsay, and Emily

Chapter 1

Brooke Conrad was excited. The first game of the high school softball season was only a week away and everything was falling nicely into place. She had already won the starting shortstop position during tryouts the week before, practices were going well, and the team was starting to gel as a unit. Her school, Silver Lake High, was a traditional softball powerhouse, having won the past five Western Conference South championships in a row, and this year looked no different. They were loaded with talent at every position. Another WesCo South title, and possibly a state championship, were within reach.

It was a routine practice at first. A little stretching and light running to warm up, then various hitting drills in the team's batting cages, then some infield work. Infield work was by far Brooke's favorite part of practice. Like all great shortstops, she played defense with a passion. She loved fielding the ball and throwing it to first as hard and as fast as she could. Nothing made her happier than hearing the sound of the ball as it exploded in the first baseman's mitt.

But then she noticed something unusual. Silver Lake's baseball coach, Daniel West, was standing along the softball field's first base foul line, about twenty feet from the first baseman, with one of his top assistants at his side. He was watching Brooke carefully.

Brooke glanced across the softball fields at the neighboring baseball fields. Silver Lake was a large school, and it had a series of athletic fields next to it, and the boys' baseball fields, both varsity and JV, were within eyesight of the girls' softball fields. The only thing separating them was a small parking lot. At first Brooke thought the boys must have been done for the day, since Coach West was normally with them during their practices, but the boys were still practicing. They were at various stations running drills with other coaches.

Coach West was a tall, lean man in his mid to late forties, with short, well-kept, graying hair and deep brown eyes. He wore white baseball pants and a sweatshirt with the school's mascot, a silver shark, printed on the front. He spoke softly to his assistant, but even at this distance Brooke could easily hear what he said.

"What do you think?" There was a hint of excitement in his voice. "I think she can do it."

The assistant hesitated, thinking about what he had been asked, then nodded.

"She looks good to me. Can she bat?"

Coach West nodded. "I watched her yesterday. She's got good power and she hits the ball consistently to all parts of the field. As far as I'm concerned, she's exactly what we need."

Brooke's softball coach, Sarah Jennings, called a break, and Brooke and the rest of the girls trotted off the field. They rounded up their water bottles and grabbed seats on the bench in their dugout.

"What's up with that?" Faith Alexander asked, motioning toward Coach West. Like Brooke, Faith was a junior. She was their starting second baseman and leadoff hitter. She was a small, thin girl with cropped hair and bangs.

"I don't get it," Naomi Smith said. Naomi was a senior, one of the oldest and tallest girls on the team. Compared to Faith, she was a giant. She had dark skin and ebony hair. "He's been here all day. The boys' team must be boring him, so he came over here to check out some real talent for a change."

They laughed.

"It's something more than that," Faith said. "He's fixated on one of us in particular."

They all looked at Brooke.

Brooke didn't know what to say, but she had noticed it, too. Coach West had been watching them all, but he had been watching her by far the most. What was up with that? Why was the coach of the school's baseball team interested in her? She wasn't even certain he knew her name.

Almost on cue, Coach Jennings walked up to Coach West and they began talking. They were on the far side of the field, and Coach Jennings had her back to them, so Brooke and the other girls couldn't hear their whole conversation, only bits and pieces of it.

"Yeah," Coach Jennings said, answering one of Coach West's questions. "She's one of my best players. I don't see why she couldn't. I'm not certain she'd want to, though. It's a pretty unusual request. What? Of course you can talk to her."

She turned and walked back to the dugout, where the girls were finishing their break and putting their water bottles back into their bags. "Everyone back on the field. Except you, Brooke. Coach West wants to talk to you."

"What's up?" Brooke asked, a bit of apprehension in her voice. There was no hiding the fact she was nervous. She had no idea what Coach West would want from her.

"I'll let him tell you. He has a proposition for you. It's a little unusual, but you'd be wise to consider it. It's a unique opportunity to say the least."

Brooke still didn't know what to think. She had known Coach Jennings since her freshman year and she'd never known her to speak in riddles. She was straightforward and forthcoming most of the time.

Coach West smiled warmly as she walked up to him. "I'm Daniel West. This is my assistant, Hugh Weller."

"It's nice to meet you," Brooke said. Like everyone at Silver Lake, she knew who he was, and she had heard he was a nice guy, but she had never met him in person before.

"I don't know if you've heard or not," he said, "but the shortstop for my team, Dwayne Harper, got kicked off the team."

Brooke's eyes widened. She had never met Dwayne Harper before, but she knew who he was. He was one of the star players on the school's baseball team. He was a senior, and last year he had been selected to the WesCo South All-Conference team. He was so good he had led Silver Lake to a third-place finish at the state's championship tournament. Word had been going around school something had happened involving him, since he hadn't been at school for a week, but no one knew exactly what.

"Dwayne got caught smoking marijuana," Coach West continued. "The athletic director suspended him for the season. So now I need a new shortstop."

Brooke raised an eyebrow. She still didn't know how this involved her.

"The only shortstops I have are too young. They're both freshman. They need at least a year on the JV team before they'll be ready to play at the varsity level. So I need you to play for me this year."

Brooke's eyes nearly popped out of their sockets the minute he said it. She couldn't believe what she had just heard.

"Me? I'm a girl."

"Shortstops are shortstops. I don't care if you're a girl or not. I need someone who can get the ball from short to first as quickly as possible, and as far as I'm concerned, now that Dwayne is gone you're the best shortstop this school's got. And I've been watching you the past couple of days and that's a great arm you've got on you. It's better than most of the boys on my team."

"Are you serious? A girl can't play on a boys' team. Can she?"

Coach West shrugged. "I don't see why not. And I think you'd like it, if you gave it a chance. But I realize this is an unusual request, so if you want some time to think about it that's fine with me. But you'd be doing me a huge favor if you did. We have a great team, with a legitimate shot at winning the state title, but we can't do it without a shortstop."

"But my team, the softball team, we need a shortstop, too. I can't play on both teams."

"True. I've already talked to Coach Jennings and she says you have a capable backup who can fill-in in your absence. She's not as good as you, of course, or I'd be talking to her right now, but Coach Jennings says she'll get the job done."

Brooke contemplated what he had said and nodded in agreement. It was true. Her backup at short, Casey Morgan, was a year younger than her, but she was a good player nonetheless. She was solid on defense, quick on the base paths, and could hit the ball almost as well as Brooke did.

Coach West smiled. "Did I mention I'm willing to make it worth your while?"

Brooke looked at him curiously.

"You girls have felt mistreated for awhile now, right? You feel like the baseball team gets all the good equipment and the nice fields. In the meantime, you get the leftovers."

Brooke nodded. Everyone knew the boys' teams at Silver Lake were treated better than the girls. That was a fact of life, and it had always been like that.

"I've already talked to the athletic director and authorized him to transfer the bulk of the baseball team's budget to the softball team this year. That way you girls can finally get that scoreboard you've always wanted."

Brooke could hardly believe what she had just heard. The softball field at Silver Lake had a small, electronic scoreboard, but it was old, rusty and rarely (if ever) worked. The girls had wanted a new one for years, and they had had several car washes to raise money to buy one, but they still didn't have nearly enough. And at the rate they were going, they wouldn't have enough until long after Brooke had graduated, which really took the fun out of it.

"Really? We get your money for the year?"

"Only on one condition. You play for me."

Brooke didn't know what to say. Her mind was on overdrive, trying to process all of the information she had been told. She wanted to help the softball team get its scoreboard, but playing for the baseball team? Could she do it? Was she good enough to play for a boys' team? And how would the boys react? Would they even want her on their team?

This was a big decision. She needed some time to think about it.

Chapter 2

"You'll be a hero," Naomi told Brooke. "You'll be known as the girl who finally got us that darn scoreboard."

They sat in the local Starbucks, just across the street from the high school's main building, eating scones and other goodies. Practice had ended twenty minutes before and Brooke was telling them about Coach West's proposition.

"You'll be a legend," Aubrey Nelson said. Aubrey was their starting third baseman. She was a sophomore, with a young face and long, straight bangs. A lot of people, including Brooke, thought she looked like Miley Cyrus. At least in some ways.

"What do you mean?" Brooke asked.

"How many girls have played on a boys' team before? You may be the first one to do it, at least at our school. You'll be making history."

"I don't care about history," Naomi said. "I just want that darn scoreboard. We've been raising money for that thing since I was a freshman. I'd like to see it before I graduate."

"Are you actually considering this?" Faith asked. Unlike the other girls, Faith wasn't excited by the idea at all. Not even the slightest.

Brooke raised an eyebrow. "A little."

"You've got to be losing your mind. A girl can't play baseball. That's why they invented softball in the first place. We're just not strong enough. Have you seen how big a baseball field is? A softball field is tiny by comparison."

"Coach West thinks I can do it. He wouldn't have asked me if he didn't. And who would know better? He's been the baseball coach here at Silver Lake for how long?"

To be perfectly honest, no one knew. All they knew was he was one of the most talented and well-respected coaches at the school, and he had led the baseball team to two state titles during his time there. There were rumors he had been offered the head coaching position at Western Washington University a few years back but had turned it down.

"I still think it's crazy," Faith said. "And what does Coach Jennings think about it?"

"I talked to her after practice for a couple of minutes," Brooke said, "just before I came over here. She didn't say much. She said it was my choice and she'd support whatever decision I made."

"We need you on our team," Faith said. "The boys can take care of themselves. If they need a shortstop, that's their problem."

"Speaking of boys," Aubrey said, "imagine that. You'll be teammates with eleven of the cutest boys at Silver Lake. And you'll be the only girl on the team, so you'll have their complete and undivided attention. I think I'd do it for that reason alone."

Brooke's eyes got big. She hadn't thought of that before.

"And you'll get to play with Alex Anderson," Naomi said.

They all sighed. Alex Anderson was undeniably the cutest boy at Silver Lake. Only Nathan O'Malley, the football team's starting quarterback, came close. Alex was a senior and was the team's star pitcher. He had been their starter since his freshman year and had already signed a letter of intent to play for the University of Washington the following spring.

"Can you imagine if he picked you up from practice in his car?" Aubrey asked.

Alex drove a silver Porsche. Next to Alex himself, it was the most gorgeous thing Brooke had ever seen.

"You three need to get serious," Faith said, snapping them back to reality. "This isn't about fancy cars or cute boys. This is about fitting in. Brooke's not going to fit in. The boys aren't going to want her on their team no matter how good she is."

"Why do you say that?" Brooke asked.

"They're just not going to. Boys' teams are for boys. Just like girls' teams are for girls. You wait and see. If you join that team, it's going to be nothing but problems for you. I guarantee it."

Brooke didn't know how to respond, so she said nothing.

"It's ridiculous," Brooke's dad said. He sat at their dining room table, finishing the last of his dinner. "Playing for a boys' team? It's the dumbest thing I've ever heard, Brooke."

Brooke's dad was an attorney at a big firm in downtown Seattle. Brooke's mom claimed most attorneys were stubborn, emotional, and completely irrational ninety-nine percent of the time, and at that particular point Brooke was definitely agreeing with her.

"But dad," she pleaded, "you haven't heard the details yet."

"Details? I don't need details. It's ridiculous. Completely ridiculous."

"Why? Don't you think I can do it? Weren't you the one who said I was going to be the best shortstop in WesCo this year?"

"I meant the best softball shortstop." He put special emphasis on the word 'softball.' "Not the best baseball shortstop."

"What's the difference?"

"They're completely different sports."

"How so?"

"There are so many differences I don't even know where to begin."

"Give it a try," Brooke said, somewhat sarcastically. If her dad wanted to be difficult, then she could be difficult, too.

"For starters," he said, "a baseball is a different size and weight than a softball. It's a lot smaller and lighter. And a baseball field is a lot bigger, the bases are further apart, there's a mound, and the players are a lot bigger and stronger. You're going to get hurt if you compete against them."

"I could get hurt playing softball."

"Not as easily." He paused for a second to take a bite of his food. "And you'll probably mess up your chances of getting into a good college."

"What? What are you talking about? Why would I mess up my chances of getting into a good college?"

"How's that going to look to college scouts? The big softball schools want softball players, Brooke. Not baseball players."

"You yourself said the big schools don't look at high school players anymore. They just look at select players. And I'll keep playing for my select team, just like I've always done. That way I can still play in college if you want."

In addition to playing for her high school team, Brooke also played for a select team called the Eastside Angels.

Her dad sighed, then took a drink from the glass in front of him. There was a long, awkward silence as he sat there, staring directly at her for what seemed like an eternity.

"You really want to do this? Have you already made up your mind?"

"Not really. But I'm leaning that way."

"Why?"

"A lot of reasons, I guess. But I think it's largely because you always tell me I should try new things, and I shouldn't be afraid to go out on a limb on occasion, and well this is a really big limb."

"Really big."

"How many people can say they've done anything like this?"

Much to her surprise, he smiled. It was a begrudging smile, but a smile nonetheless. "I will admit I like your attitude, Brooke. I always wanted you to feel like you could take on the world, but I still think this is a terrible idea. Something bad is going to happen. I just know it."

"So you won't let me? You won't let me play?"

"I didn't say that. How old are you now?"

"Sixteen."

"Sixteen? How did you get so old so fast? It seems like just yesterday you were crawling around on the floor in your diapers. Those were good times. Not the diapers, but the crawling on the floor part. Anyway, you're old enough now to make your own decisions, at least some of them. But don't come running back to me when this whole thing blows up in your face. And this better not interfere with your select team in any way or there'll be hell to pay. I paid good money for the select team and I really like watching you play on it. So don't mess it up. Understood?"

Brooke nodded.

Without another word, he finished his dinner, stood up, and left the room.

Brooke hardly slept that night. The idea of playing on the baseball team was ludicrous.

Even she had to admit it. She had played softball for as long as she could remember, and she was undeniably one of the best players in the county, but her dad was right. Baseball and softball were two completely different sports, and each required its own set of skills. There was no reason to think she would excel at baseball just because she excelled at softball. If she were smart, she'd forget the whole idea, go back to her softball team and have another great season like she'd always done in the past. But for some strange reason, some reason she couldn't put into words, she just couldn't get the idea of playing baseball out of her mind no matter how hard she tried. She had always been the adventurous type, and she had always liked trying new and exciting things, no matter how difficult they were. That attitude had gotten her in trouble a few times in the past (like the time she tried a science experiment in the garage and nearly blew up her dad's car), but, like it or not, she was who she was.

As such, she flipped and flopped around in her bed for most of the night, until finally, at exactly 4:31 am, she made her final decision. From that point on, it was official. She was a baseball player.

Chapter 3

The baseball team was gathered together in a large group on one side of the infield as Coach West led Brooke up to them. Their chatter came to an abrupt end as he called them to attention and addressed them.

"Thanks for gathering together so quickly, guys. I'd like to introduce you to our new shortstop. Some of you may already know her from school. Her name's Brooke Conrad."

Brooke had never felt so tiny in her entire life. All of the boys, the entire team, stared at her with blank looks on their faces. No one said a word.

"Brooke was the starting shortstop for the school's softball team last year," Coach West continued. "She made the All-WesCo team. Not bad for a sophomore, if you ask me. And she also plays for one of the state's elite select teams, the Eastside Angels 18Gold team. Last year they won metros, finished second at state and seventh at nationals."

The boys remained quiet. Brooke's accolades as a softball player didn't appear to impress them much. Finally, the first baseman, a large senior named Blake Henry, spoke up.

"Coach. That's not a shortstop. That's a girl."

He said the word 'girl' as though it were dirty.

"Is this a joke?" the catcher asked. Like Blake, he was a senior, and he was the heaviest kid on the team by far. His name was Logan Sullivan but everyone called him Skinny. "You're trying to punk us, right coach? Like last year when you said you were going to give us a day off, then you made us run wind sprints the whole practice instead?"

Coach West smiled. "That was a fun day. I've never seen anyone puke that much before, Skinny. But no, this is no joke. Brooke is our new shortstop. She's on loan from the softball team for a year."

"You've got to be kidding," Blake said. "I bet she can't even throw the ball all the way to first."

"Let's find out," Coach West said. "Everyone take your positions."

The boys, still somewhat mystified by what had happened, grabbed their gear and headed to their positions in the field. Brooke hesitated for a second. She hadn't expected them to react this way and, as such, she didn't know what to do.

"Just give them a chance," Coach West told her. "They'll come around. I hope."

The 'I hope' part didn't make Brooke feel much better, but not knowing what else to do, she grabbed her mitt and jogged out to short. It was at that point she actually stopped and looked around for the first time. She had never been on a baseball field before, and she had never realized how much bigger a baseball field was than a softball field. From her position at short, first base seemed like it was a mile away. Even Blake, as big and as strong as he was, looked small all the way over there. She started to wonder if he was right. Could she throw the ball all the way to him?

The problem was actually the opposite. The bases were a long way apart, but the issue was not the distance at all. The issue was the ball. As her dad had said the night before, a baseball was a lot smaller and lighter than a softball. Brooke fielded the first ball that was hit to her, but then dropped it in the dirt.

Lesson #1: Gripping a baseball is a lot different than gripping a softball.

Blake laughed the minute she dropped the ball.

"It's okay," Coach West said. "Try it again, Brooke. Keep your eyes on the ball at all times."

He hit her another grounder. Once again, she fielded it cleanly, and this time she actually managed to transfer it to her throwing hand without any problems. But this time the problem was the throw. She threw it over Blake's head and into the bushes at the far side of the field.

Lesson #2: A baseball flies a lot further than a softball.

"Nice aim," Skinny smirked.

"That's okay," Coach West said. "Try it again, Brooke. Nice and easy this time."

From that point forward, things got a little better, but not much. On her next attempt, she overcompensated and threw the ball too low. It hit the dirt at Blake's feet, shot upward, and nailed him in the shin.

"You trying to kill me?"

Her next throw was a little better, but wide to the right, her next throw was wide to the left, and her next throw was too high again. Coach West tried to help her by mixing things up, and he hit a ball to the second baseman, a junior named Jamie Stephens.

"Turn two," Coach West called.

Jamie turned and fired the ball to second.

It would have been a great play. The only problem was Brooke was nowhere near second when the ball got there. She had miscalculated how long it would take to get to second and hadn't arrived in time. The ball flew into left field.

Lesson #3: There is a lot more territory to cover on a baseball field.

Blake laughed. "What, they don't cover second in softball?"

"Try it again, Brooke," Coach West called. "Faster this time. You can do it."

The second play went a little better than the first. Brooke got to the base in time, but once again her throw to Blake was wild. And so was the throw after that, and the one after that, and the one after that.

Brooke had never been so relieved to have a practice come to an end. She was completely frustrated and embarrassed by her performance. She had never played so poorly in her entire life, even back in her Little League days, when she was young and just learning the basics. She rounded up her belongings as quickly as she could, loaded them into her softball bag, and hurried to her car in the adjoining parking lot.

She cried the whole way home.

Chapter 4

Practice the next day didn't get much better. If anything, it got worse. Brooke continued to struggle in the field, and she started doing the one thing players were taught to never do. She started aiming the ball. Any good player knew you didn't aim the ball; you just threw it. The minute you started aiming it, chaos began. And for Brooke, it was complete chaos. One throw went high, another went higher, the next even higher. And the worst thing was the harder she tried, the worse it got. Blake shook his head as an errant throw soared over his head and disappeared into the bushes.

"At this rate," he said, "we're going to be out of balls by our first game."

Brooke didn't do any better batting. She couldn't believe how much heavier a baseball bat was than a softball bat. And the helmets didn't have facemasks. That was downright scary. What would happen if a pitch came at her head, or even worse, her face? But the thing that worried her the most was the speed of the pitches. Most high school baseball pitchers threw around eighty miles per hour;

most softball pitchers around sixty. She was afraid she wouldn't be able to hit the ball because it was travelling so much faster than she was used to. But it was actually the opposite. Since a baseball pitcher stood so far away from the plate, it actually negated the increase in velocity and made the ball take much longer to get there. Which was actually a bad thing for Brooke, since she was the type of hitter who liked the ball to get to her quickly. She missed the first nine pitches completely before she managed to finally make contact and foul one to the side.

"Darn," Skinny said, removing his catcher's mask. "You just cost me five bucks."

"What?" Brooke asked, turning to face him.

"I bet Jamie five bucks you wouldn't make contact all day."

Brooke let out a sigh, dug her cleats into the dirt, and tried again. Unfortunately, Skinny's words had rattled her even worse than she already was, and she didn't do well at all. She fouled two more pitches away, but that was the best she could do. As she walked back to the dugout, ending her turn, she shot a quick glance at the distant fields where the softball team was practicing. She watched as Aubrey scooped up a grounder and zipped it to Naomi at first. Faith ran over and patted her on the back. It was a sweet play. All three girls were nothing but smiles.

Brooke, by contrast, had forgotten how to smile.

The ultimate humiliation, however, came after practice. As Brooke walked back to her car, completely lost in her thoughts, someone grabbed her from behind and spun her around. It was Blake. He was even bigger and more menacing up close than he was from a distance. Skinny was at his side, as was Terrell Williams, their center fielder, and Aiden Andrews, their left fielder.

"Are you ready to quit yet?" Blake asked.

"What?" Brooke asked.

"I said," he repeated. "Are you ready to quit yet?"

Brooke didn't know what to say so she remained silent.

"Catch a clue. We don't want you here. A girl doesn't belong on a boys' team. Got it?"

Brooke still didn't know what to say, so she said nothing.

Blake got frustrated by her lack of a response. "So be it. But if you're going to play on a boys' team, then you're going to be treated like a boy. And that means wearing one of these, just like the rest of us."

He held up his free hand, revealing an old, discolored jockstrap. The sight of it made Brooke recoil in shock. Unfortunately, she couldn't do anything, including move away, since Blake had her with his other hand.

"Hold her still for me," he told the other boys.

Skinny, Terrell, and Aidan grabbed her and held her in place. She tried to pull free but couldn't budge an inch. She was by far the smallest of them all, and any one of the boys could have held her in place by himself, let alone all three at once.

The boys laughed as Blake raised the jockstrap into the air and pulled it down over her head. Brooke's heart raced and she called out for help but nobody was nearby to hear her.

"You want to be one of the boys?" Blake asked. "Now you're one of the boys."

Without another word, they released her, turned, and walked away, laughing hysterically as they went. Skinny patted Blake on the back. In the meantime, and as fast as she could, Brooke tore the jockstrap from her head, threw it to the side, and ran straight to her car, locking the doors as soon as she got inside.

The day before, she hadn't started crying until after she had started the car and begun driving home. On that day, she didn't wait that long. The tears were flowing before she got her key in the ignition.

Chapter 5

"I'm quitting the team."

Brooke had arrived at practice a few minutes early so she could tell Coach West before the boys arrived. After what had happened the day before, with Blake and the jockstrap, she couldn't take it anymore. She hated to admit it, but her dad had been right. A girl wasn't meant to play on a boys' team and she had learned it the hard way. Now the only thing left to do was admit she had been wrong and rectify her mistake.

"Why?" Coach West asked. "You're doing fine."

"I can't throw. Or field. Or hit. I'm terrible."

"We all have bad days. You need to be patient. You're a great athlete, Brooke. You'll get it. You just need time to adjust."

She decided to cut to the chase. To give him the real reason she was quitting the team.

"The boys don't want me here. I'm doing them a favor by leaving."

"Boys are boys, Brooke. You need to give them a chance. Give them a little time and they'll come around. They just need to see what you're capable of. Once they do, they'll accept you."

She was tempted to tell him about the night before, but she was much too ashamed and embarrassed. In addition, she didn't want to risk upsetting the boys (especially Blake and Skinny) any more. If they found out she had ratted on them, she'd have even more issues than she already did.

"It's up to you, Brooke," Coach West said. "I'm not going to force you to do anything you don't want to. And I apologize if this has been tough on you. But please do me a favor. Give it until Friday. That's only two more days. If you're still uncomfortable by then, I understand completely."

She didn't really want to, she wanted the whole ordeal to be over immediately, but she nodded and turned to head to the dugout. She only got one step before Coach West's voice stopped her momentarily.

"I really appreciate what you've done. Regardless of how this turns out, even if you leave the team for good on Friday, you girls are still getting that scoreboard. I give you my word."

Blake, Skinny, and the other boys were amazed to see her at practice when they arrived. Clearly, they thought they had scared her off and had seen the last of her. But then, once they realized she was there, they got worried, worried she had told Coach West about the night before, and they shot her menacing looks. When Coach West said nothing about it and started practice like any other day, they settled down a little. They didn't say anything to her, and they stayed pretty much to themselves, but that was fine with her. Actually, it was exactly what she wanted. She needed to focus on baseball and baseball alone, and she didn't need any distractions.

And then something completely unexpected happened. She got an ally.

Or at least someone who wasn't hostile.

During infield drills, Coach West hit a ball up the middle of the field. It should have been a single, but Brooke got a good jump on it and got to it quickly, scooped it up, and made a decent throw to first.

"Nice play," Jamie said as he walked past her. He was the second baseman. He, too, had been after the ball, but Brooke had gotten to it first and had made the play for him.

It was the first compliment Brooke had received as a baseball player. And amazingly, it made all the difference in the world. After that, she could make plays again. Just like she did in softball. Well, not quite that well, since she was still getting used to the feel of the ball in her hand (it still felt so light), but finally she could do it. Her throws got better and better, and as her confidence improved, she started putting some real zip on them. Blake rubbed his hand as she whipped a throw to first and it hit him in the palm. He shot her a quick glance, but for the first time it was a glance of admiration, not disdain. Clearly, he had never expected her to be able to throw a ball quite that hard.

Batting practice was a similar story. She finally got her timing down, and she was able to make contact with the pitches regularly. She still didn't hit too many balls all that well, but one of her shots got all of their attention. She sent one ball all the way to the outfield warning track. The center fielder, Terrell, caught it, with his back against the wall, but it was a nice hit anyway.

Especially for a girl.

Chapter 6

Coach West rounded them up before the beginning of Friday's practice.

"As you know, Monday is our first game, so today is our last practice before the season officially begins. So I want everyone to give a little extra today. Monday's game is against Monroe, so it's not a league game, but I want to win it anyway. And we're going to need to be sharp, because Monroe is a solid team. They finished second in WesCo North last year, and word is they got a new pitcher who's pretty tough."

"He's no match for Alex," Skinny said, patting their star pitcher on the back.

It was at that point Brooke got her first chance to look at Alex Anderson. Like all of the boys, he had been at practice every day that week, but Brooke had been so preoccupied with her struggles she had hardly even noticed him. And she could hardly believe she hadn't. He was perfect in every way. Tall and lean, with slightly ruffled, dirty blond hair. His eyes were the deepest blue Brooke had ever seen. She was mesmerized just looking at them.

"That may be true," Coach West said, "but I don't want to take anything for granted. We need to get off to a good start this year. Since we're the defending South champions, everyone's going to be gunning for us, so we need to send a quick message to the rest of the league. Am I being clear?"

They all nodded.

"So let's start with some running."

They all groaned but took their places on the first base foul line. One of the assistant coaches placed orange cones at various distances from the line, and they had to run from the foul line to the first cone, then back to the foul line, then to the next cone, then back to the foul line, and so on. They took off on Coach West's word. Brooke ran as fast as she could but was quickly left behind. Even the slowest of the boys (Skinny and Blake) were faster than she was, and by quite a bit. She was both shocked and dismayed. On her softball teams, she had always been at the front of the pack.

After running, they did infield. She struggled a bit initially and threw one ball into the dirt at Blake's feet, but then settled down and did well. After infield, they switched to batting, but unlike the previous day, she started struggling again.

"You're trying too hard," Jamie said. He stood in the on-deck circle, waiting for his turn to bat. "A baseball is a lot lighter than a softball. You don't need to hit it so hard. Just focus on making contact. If you hit it square, it will rebound for a base hit. Maybe more."

Much to Brooke's delight, he was right. She cut down the power and intensity in her swings and instead focused exclusively on making good, solid contact. Almost instantly she got results, and they were good results. After awhile, she was even doing simple check-swings and still hitting the ball sharply through the infield.

"Thanks," she said as she ended her turn and headed back to the dugout.

"No problem," he said with a smile.

As she stood in the dugout removing her batting gloves, she thought about the various boys on the team. Jamie was the only one so far who had been friendly to her. Blake, Skinny, and most of the other boys had been hostile. But there was one boy she still had no idea about, and he was the one she was the most interested in.

Alex.

He hadn't said a word to her all week. Not a thing, good, bad, or otherwise. She wondered where he stood regarding having her on the team.

She didn't get much time to think about it, however. Coach West walked up and interrupted her thoughts.

"Nice hitting. That's the best I've seen you do all week."

"Thanks."

"So what's it going to be?"

She looked at him quizzically. She had no idea what he was talking about.

"Today is Friday. I asked you to wait until today to make your decision about quitting the team. Have you made it?"

Brooke was completely caught off guard. Two days prior, she had completely, adamantly wanted off the team. But now, a mere forty-eight hours later, she wasn't so sure. She was finally starting to get the hang of this baseball thing, and the boys (even Blake and Skinny) hadn't been quite as rude toward her since the incident with the jockstrap. And one of the boys, Jamie, even seemed friendly.

"I'm not sure."

"I thought you'd say that. How about if we make another deal? How about if you give it a few more days? That way you'll have a chance to try some games. And I think you'll really like the games."

She didn't know what to say, so she simply nodded. She had a habit of doing that.

Whenever she didn't know what to do, she just went with the flow.

"Good," Coach West said. "In that case, for Monday's game, you'll be starting at short, but I'm going to bat you last in the order. I know some players get offended when they have to bat last, but I want you to know I'm only doing it because you're the new kid on the team. If you bat well in a couple of games, I'll move you up accordingly."

To be perfectly honest, Brooke wasn't offended at all. Quite to the contrary, she was relieved. Batting last in the order would cut down on her total number of at-bats, which would take a lot of pressure off of her. Instead of focusing so much on batting, she could put the majority of her attention on her fielding.

And right then, she needed as little pressure as possible.

Chapter 7

The following weekend, Brooke's select softball team had a tournament in Bellevue, a city about fifteen minutes east of Seattle. Brooke played for the Eastside Angels 18Gold team, a team made up primarily of sixteen, seventeen, and eighteen-year-old girls from all over the Seattle metropolitan area. Several of Brooke's teammates from school, including Faith, Aubrey, and Naomi, were also on the team. Brooke had played for the Angels for three years. Originally, she hadn't liked it too much, since they wore white and pink uniforms that were way too 'girly' for her, but her dad had insisted she join since it was one of the most prestigious teams in the area. And after a while she got used to the uniforms and even liked them a little, especially their logo, which was the letter "E" with a gold halo around its upper left edge.

Their first game was against a team from Redmond called the LadyCats, and it started off poorly. The LadyCats' shortstop, who was a tall, lean girl named Kiana Cruise, hit a ground ball to Brooke's left, but Brooke read it wrong and it skipped past her for a single.

It had been awhile since she had been on a softball field. She had forgotten how much smaller it was than a baseball field and how quickly a grounder could get to and past her.

"Come on, Brooke," her dad called. Like always, he sat with the other parents in the bleachers. "Adjust your angles. Read the ball better. You know better."

Unfortunately, it didn't get much better from there. In the second inning, another LadyCat batter hit a grounder to her. Unlike the one hit by Kiana, she grabbed it easily, but then threw it into the dirt at Naomi's feet. She had forgotten how heavy a softball was and hadn't put enough power behind it. Luckily for her, Naomi made a great play and dug it out of the dirt for the final out to finish the inning.

"Don't worry about it," Naomi said as they sat in the dugout. "You'll get it back. Just be patient."

"Here's what I want to know," Aubrey said, sitting down on the bench next to Brooke. She had her batting helmet in one hand and a package of sunflower seeds in the other. "What's it like being teammates with Alex? Is he as hot as everyone says?"

Brooke smiled. "He's pretty hot."

Aubrey raised an eyebrow. "Pretty hot?"

"He's incredibly hot," Brooke said, correcting herself.

They laughed.

"So have you spoken to him yet?" Faith asked.

Brooke hesitated. "Well, not really, but I think he looked at me once."

"He looked at you?" Aubrey asked. "Oh my God. You're the luckiest girl in the world."

Faith looked at Aubrey and shook her head in disgust. "Would you shut up for a minute?" She turned to Brooke. "Let me get this straight. You've been on the team for a week, practiced with them every day, but he hasn't said a single thing to you?"

"Boys are different than girls. They don't talk too much during practice. Well, at least not to me."

"What does that mean?" Faith asked.

"Let's just say I'm still trying to fit in." Brooke didn't really know how to explain it any better than that, and to be perfectly honest, she didn't really want to. And under no circumstances was she going to tell them about the incident with Blake, Skinny, and the jockstrap. She would die before she would let anyone know about that.

"But there is this one boy," she continued. "He talks to me and he's been pretty nice so far. His name is Jamie."

"Jamie Stephens?" Naomi asked. "The junior?"

"Yeah. Do you know him?"

"He's in my English class. He's really nice. A good student, too. He always does his homework and he knows most of the answers whenever Mr. Wilson calls on him. Which is a lot more than I can say."

They all laughed. It was common knowledge Naomi had homework issues. Let's just say the words 'Naomi' and 'homework' were rarely used in the same sentence unless the sentence was, 'Naomi didn't do her homework last night.'

"What do you know about him?" Brooke asked. Until she had joined the baseball team, she had never met Jamie before and she was curious to learn a little more about him.

"Not much, really," Naomi said. "I heard he had a girlfriend for a while, Jessie Hines, but they broke up. Not certain why. And I think his dad is an accountant or something like that. They live on the west side of town, near the mall."

"Do you like him?" Aubrey asked. "Are you going to try to hook up with him?"

Brooke laughed. "I don't know about that. I just met him, and I barely even know anything about him. I'm the one asking you for info."

She didn't get to say anything further. One of the Angels' assistant coaches interrupted from the far end of the dugout.

"Brooke," he called, a look of desperation on his face. "Where are you? You're up."

She jumped up, grabbed her bat and helmet, and darted for the batter's box.

This happened sometimes. Sometimes, the girls got so busy talking (usually about boys) they completely forgot a game was being played.

Unfortunately, her at-bat was not a good one. She was still getting used to playing softball again, and the pitches seemed like they were lightning fast. The minute they left the pitcher's hand, they exploded in the catcher's mitt. She swung and missed three straight times.

"Eyes on the ball," her dad called from the stands. From the tone of his voice, it was clear he wasn't happy.

Luckily, despite her struggles, the team did okay and they won 6-2. Their next game, however, was a completely different story. They played a team from Federal Way called the Skyhawks. The Skyhawks were an impressive group with a lot of talented players, including their pitcher, who was a feisty girl named Riley Westmore, their shortstop, who was a small, thin girl named Erin Williams, and their center fielder, who was a young phenom named Melody Gold. Brooke was no match for them, not at all. She struck out once and grounded out twice. Both of her grounders were weak ones right to their second baseman. She was out by a mile each time.

As a result, the car ride home was deathly silent for the first ten minutes.

"What was that?" her dad asked.

"What do you mean?" she responded.

"What was up with your performance today? That was the worst I've seen you play in years. Hitless in six at-bats, with four strikeouts? And an error in the field? That's not like you at all. You're usually the star. Not the goat."

Brooke sighed. "I had an off day. It won't happen again."

"It better not. It's this baseball thing, isn't it? It's throwing you off. Your timing, your angles. You looked like you didn't know what you were doing out there today. Like you'd never played the game before."

Brooke cringed. She couldn't believe he had figured out the cause of her problems so quickly.

"I just need time to adjust. I'll get it back. You'll see."

"For your sake, I better see it soon."

Unfortunately, he didn't see it the next day. The Angels won all three of their games, but Brooke continued to struggle, both at the plate and in the field. She got one hit, a single during the final game, but that was it for her highlights. In the meantime, she made two errors at short. Both were wild throws at Naomi's feet.

"See," her dad said as they drove home. "I was right. I knew this baseball thing was a bad idea."

Brooke didn't know what to say, so she remained silent the whole drive home. It was one of the most awkward, unpleasant car rides they had ever had, and it was a complete departure from the norm. Normally, the car ride home was great fun and they spent the whole time talking about how well she had done that day.

Chapter 8

Brooke was nervous.   It was her first game as a baseball player, and she needed to do well to prove to the boys she belonged on the team.   But that wasn't the only reason she was nervous.   She was also nervous because something unexpected happened.

Her dad showed up.   Since he didn't approve of her whole 'baseball thing' she had assumed he wouldn't come.   But he had.   She stopped by the bleachers to say hi.

"I didn't expect to see you today."

"I may not like this," he responded.   "But you're still my daughter, so I'm here to give you what support I can.   But do me a favor, okay?   Try not to embarrass yourself too much."

She recoiled instantly.   The words cut right through her, right to her core.   As she took her place at short to start the game, she could barely keep the tears out of her eyes.

Her dad could be such a jerk at times. She hated him.   If it was the last thing she would do, she'd prove him wrong.   She was going to make this baseball thing work just to spite him.

Unfortunately, things did not start well. The game was against Monroe and their leadoff batter hit the first pitch straight at her. She fielded it on a hop but rushed the throw and sent it soaring into a distant light pole. The ball bounced off the pole, hit the side of the bleachers, and ended up in a pool of water in a nearby ditch.

Blake shook his head in dismay.

Jamie walked up to her as the next batter took his place in the batter's box and started his warm-up swings.

"This may make things worse," he said, "and I hate it whenever people say it to me, but I've got to say it anyway. You need to relax. Everything will be okay if you relax. So just forget that last one and get the next one. Okay?"

It wasn't easy, but she forced herself to do just that. She blocked out everything she could – Blake, Skinny, her dad, everything unpleasant, and just played ball. And, much to her relief, it worked. The second batter popped out to Terrell in center, the batter after that lined out to Jamie at second, and the batter after that hit a lazy grounder to her at short. She rushed in, grabbed it on the run, and made a nice, easy throw to Blake to end the inning.

Despite her error to start the game, no damage had been done, and now it was their turn to bat. And they took advantage of the opportunity immediately. Jamie led off with a single to right, Terrell sacrificed him to second with a fly ball to left, and then he scored when Alex hit a single straight up the middle. Blake followed Alex's single with one of his own, and Alex, who was extremely fast for a pitcher, scored all of the way from first.

Just like that, and much to everyone's delight, they were ahead 2-0.

Coach West rounded them up before they returned to the field to begin the second inning.

"That was a nice start, boys." He took a quick glance at Brooke, then added, "And girl. Now let's keep it up. Good defense."

They all started to head onto the field, but he stopped Brooke briefly so he could address her personally. "I like what I saw out there, Brooke. I don't care about an error on occasion. I care about how you respond when you make one. Keep your chin up and keep playing hard at all times. Effort and attitude win championships. Understood?"

"Yes, sir."

The score remained 2-0 until Brooke's first at-bat in the bottom of the third. Monroe's pitcher was a freshman, but he was extremely big for his age and he threw really hard. Brooke had never faced a pitcher who threw that hard before. He struck her out with three straight fastballs. She swung at all three, but her swings were low and late each time.

"It's okay," Coach West said as she trotted back to the dugout. "You'll get it next time."

Unfortunately, she didn't. She finally managed to make contact, and she fouled one pitch away, but that was the best she could do. As such, she struck out for the second time in as many attempts.

But her third at-bat, in the bottom of the sixth inning, was another story. They were still leading 2-0 and they had runners on second and third with two outs. Brooke knew if she could get a hit, even something as weak as a bloop single, both runs would score and the game would likely be over. Monroe had only gotten two hits off of Alex all day, one in the second inning and one in the fourth, and he wasn't showing any signs of letting up. Monroe's pitcher, however, was beginning to struggle. His brow was covered in sweat and he was clearly tiring. The velocity of his fastball had dipped significantly in recent innings.

This is my chance, Brooke thought as she stepped into the batter's box. She tapped her bat on the plate, measuring the distance to it carefully. She dug her cleats into the dirt. Her hands shook with anticipation.

The first pitch was down and away for ball one.

"Good eye," her dad called from the stands.

The second pitch was even lower. Ball two.

This was it. Brooke knew the logistics of batting well, and she knew Monroe's pitcher wouldn't want to throw her another ball. No pitcher ever wanted to go 3-0. As such, he was likely to do anything possible to get a strike, including something as stupid as throwing the ball straight down the middle of the plate. And, exactly as she had predicted, he did. Brooke had already started her swing even before the ball came out of his hand, and she hit it straight back at him. It went right over his shoulder and into center field for a single. Silver Lake's dugout erupted in cheers and they all jumped to their feet as the runners came around to score. Monroe's center fielder grabbed the ball but didn't even try a throw to the plate. He knew that even if he did his throw would be way too late.

As Brooke stood on first base, catching her breath, she couldn't have been happier. Despite all she had gone through the past week, the frustrations, the embarrassments, and the tears, she had done it. She had persevered, and in so doing, she had gotten her first big hit as a baseball player.

They won 4-0.

Chapter 9

Their second game, which was against a school called Meadowdale, was more of the same for Brooke. She was nervous at first, and things were made even worse by the opposing coach. The minute she stepped into the batter's box for her first at-bat, he called a timeout and rushed onto the field.

"What's up with this? Girls can't play baseball."

"Why do you say that?" the umpire responded.

"Look at her. She's tiny. She's gonna get hurt for sure."

The umpire shrugged. "I was the field ump during her first game. She did fine. She had several really nice throws, and a great running catch."

"There's got to be a rule against it."

"Not that I know of. So unless you've got a rulebook and can point to something, let's get this show back on the road."

Meadowdale's coach didn't know what else to say, and he didn't want to make any more of a scene than he'd already done, so he returned to his dugout and the game continued from there. Unfortunately, as was the case in her first game against Monroe, Brooke struck out quickly during her initial at-bat. Meadowdale's pitcher didn't throw as hard as Monroe's pitcher, but he had a nasty curveball that fooled her badly for strike three.

In the field, however, she played well. She made three nice plays in the first four innings and assisted on another. By the time she had her second at-bat in the fourth inning, they were leading 1-0. Their lone run came courtesy of a massive home run by Blake in the bottom of the second. Blake was a big boy, and he hit like it. The ball went so far it cleared the outfield fence and hit a building on the other side of the parking lot.

Brooke dug her cleats into the dirt and waited anxiously for the pitch. It was a fastball, and she fouled it away.

"Hands up," her dad shouted from the stands.

She did as instructed, kept her hands up nice and high, like her coaches and batting instructors had always taught her, and lined the next pitch down the first base foul line for a single.

She was all smiles as she stepped on first base. Unfortunately, she didn't get to smile for long. Jamie lined the next pitch all the way to the outfield wall, so she was instantly back in action, and she advanced all the way to third.   Alex followed Jamie's hit by sending a long fly ball to the outfield warning track. Meadowdale's center fielder ran under and caught it.

Coach West stood in the coach's box next to third base.

"Tag and go," he said.

Brooke reacted instantly.   She touched third base and raced for home as fast as she could.   The center fielder whipped the ball home, an awesome throw that reached the catcher at the exact same second Brooke got there. The catcher was so intent on grabbing the ball he never saw how close Brooke was, and Brooke was so intent on getting to home plate she never saw how close the catcher was. The ensuing collision was so violent it knocked Brooke completely off her feet and onto her back, and it instantly took the wind out of her lungs. She had never felt anything like it before.   It was like she had run headfirst into a brick wall.

But luckily for her, her pain was quickly forgotten.   Although Meadowdale's catcher had stayed on his feet, the impact from the collision had jarred him just enough to make him drop the ball. It was lying to the side, just a few feet away from Brooke's head, in the dirt. In the meantime, Brooke was lying flat on her back, but she was lying right on top of home plate.

The umpire took one look at the scenario and made an instant decision. "Safe!"

The fans in the bleachers, including her dad, cheered loudly, and her teammates rushed out to congratulate her and make certain she was okay. Coach West and Jamie helped her up and back to their dugout. The team's athletic trainer got her an icepack and put it on her neck, fearing she had suffered a bad case of whiplash as a result of the collision and the ensuing fall. As she sat there, on the bench in the dugout trying to catch her breath and regain her senses, she couldn't help but overhear several of the boys, including Terrell and Skinny, who were talking at the far end of the dugout.

"That catcher is a monster," Terrell said. "I can't believe she took him on. I'd never go near that guy."

"I'll give her credit," Skinny said. "She may be small, but she's as brave as they get."

Brooke raised an eyebrow. Compliments from Skinny and Terrell? She never thought she'd see the day.

Chapter 10

Brooke's dad handed her an icepack as she sat on the couch. It was the third one she had used that night.

"What were you thinking?" He had a frustrated but concerned look on his face. "You're 5'2", 125 pounds when you're soaking wet. That catcher was like 6' tall, and who knows how heavy. You could have been killed."

"It just happened so quickly," Brooke said. Her body ached everywhere, and she felt like she had been hit by a bus. "I didn't really mean to run into him. I was going to slide but he was blocking the plate."

"You nearly gave me a heart attack." He plopped down next to her. "And I thought all those years of softball were stressful. This baseball is ten times worse. It's going to be the death of me."

He took the icepack from her and placed it on his forehead.

Brooke chuckled. Her dad could be extremely difficult at times, but he usually came around sooner or later, if she just gave him enough time. Was this going to be one of those times?

"I'll give credit where credit is due," he said. "You hit that catcher the second the ball got there. It's no wonder he dropped it. And boy were you flying down the line. That's the fastest I've seen you run in years. It reminded me of that game a few years back when you scored the winning run against the Washington Wildcats. When you slid under the catcher's tag."

Brooke remembered it well. "That was a fun game. One of the best ever."

"You can say that again." He thought for a minute then continued. "That was a nice single you had today. And yesterday. I'll be honest, I didn't think you could do it, but you did. Two hits in two days. That's not bad. Not bad at all. Especially for a rookie."

They sat in silence for several minutes before he spoke again.

"Are you absolutely committed to this baseball thing?"

She thought about it for a second, then said, "I think so. It's not easy, there's no doubt about that, but I think I can do it if everyone will just give me a chance. And when I say everyone, that means you, dad."

She put extra emphasis on the word 'dad.'

He let out a loud, remorseful sigh. "This is the hardest part of being a parent. Sometimes you've got to let your kids do things you don't like. I'm still not happy about it, not one bit, but I'll do my best to support you from now on, if that's what you want. And I promise I won't make any more comments like the one I made at the Monroe game. That was totally inappropriate and I regretted it the minute I said it. But my support is on one condition."

She wrinkled her brow and looked at him. "What?"

"Stay away from 6' tall catchers from now on."

Brooke laughed and gave him a hug. "I'll do my best."

Chapter 11

Brooke sat in the school cafeteria eating lunch with Naomi, Faith, and Aubrey. It had been two days since the game against Meadowdale, but she was still a little sore from her collision with Meadowdale's catcher.

"How's it going?" Naomi asked. "Things getting better with the team?"

"A little. I think the players have started to warm up to me a little. Yesterday at practice, Terrell and Aiden said hi as I got there. And JJ said, "Nice," after I made a play. And Jamie talks to me a lot, but he's never been a problem."

"What's up with that?" Naomi asked.

"I'm not sure. He met me after practice last night, at my car, and we spoke for a while. Nothing serious, just small talk, but it was kind of nice. It's the first time I've talked to one of the boys off the field."

"Enough of this," Aubrey interrupted. There was clear irritation in her voice. "Jamie's nice and all, but come on. You know who we want to hear about. Alex. Any luck with him?"

Brooke smiled. "Not really. He's tough to read. He stays to himself most of the time, and he's really focused and serious during practice."

"That's 'cause of his dad," Aubrey said.

"What?" the girls asked in unison.

"His dad is pretty tough on him. He's pushed him really hard over the years, ever since he was little. That's probably why he's so good now. But let me get this straight. He doesn't speak to anyone during practice?"

"Of course he does," Brooke said, "and all the other guys really like him, but he doesn't say much. And he's never said anything to me, good, bad, or otherwise. To be perfectly honest I don't know if he even knows I exist."

"Most pitchers know their shortstops exist," Faith said.

"You know what I mean. I don't know if he wants me on the team or not. I assume he does, since he's never made any objections, but it's hard to say. Right now, he seems pretty indifferent."

"You know what I heard?" Aubrey said. "There's a rumor going around school. It's a doozie."

Aubrey was their main source of gossip. If anyone in their group ever had big news, true or false, it was always her.

"What?" they asked in unison.

"I heard he's having issues with Alyssa."

Brooke's heart skipped a beat the minute she said it. Alyssa Allen was Alex's girlfriend. She was a senior and was a star player on Silver Lake's volleyball team. She and Alex had been a couple since they were sophomores. This past year, as seniors, they had been homecoming king and queen.

"What kind of problems?"

"Let's just say Alyssa went to a movie with someone else last week."

"Really?" they all asked. "Who?"

"I never found out. No one knows for certain, and as you can imagine, Alyssa won't say much."

Brooke could hardly believe it. Could it be true?

"Anyway," Aubrey continued, "Alex found out about it and he wasn't happy. There's speculation they're going to break up soon. Maybe next week."

Naomi turned to Brooke. "This could be your big chance."

"What?"

"You're the only girl on the baseball team. You spend two hours a day with him, more on game days. That's more time than any other girl at this school gets with him."

"But he doesn't even speak to me. He hasn't said a single thing to me in over a week."

"That may change. Especially if he and Alyssa break up."

"This is ridiculous," Faith said. "No offense, Brooke, but he ain't going to go for you. The minute he breaks up with Alyssa, he's going to go for a cheerleader. Boys as hot as Alex always go for cheerleaders."

"But he didn't," Aubrey said. "His girlfriend is Alyssa. She's a volleyball player. Not a cheerleader. And his girlfriend before that, Amanda Tsujikawa, was a basketball player."

They sat there in silence for a minute, eating their lunches. No one, including Brooke, knew how to respond to that, and no one said a thing. Aubrey was right. Alex was the hottest boy in school by far. He could have had his choice of any girl at Silver Lake, including any of the mega-hot, high maintenance cheerleaders, but instead he had chosen a volleyball player. Alyssa was a pretty girl, there was no mistaking that, but she was far from being the most attractive girl in school. Maybe Alex was one of those strange, extremely rare boys who was attracted to something other than a pretty face. Brooke could never be that lucky.

Chapter 12

As far as Brooke was concerned, Friday's practice was awesome. Well, not the practice itself, but afterward. Jamie met her in the parking lot next to her car. She was still loading her bag into the trunk when he walked up. Like always, he was in a jovial mood and had a welcoming smile on his face.

"Good job today," he said.

She closed the trunk. "Thanks."

"You seem like you're really getting the hang of this baseball thing. You did great in batting practice. That was the best I've ever seen you hit."

"I'm getting a lot more comfortable now. Now that we've played a couple games, and I did okay, I don't feel so much pressure to prove myself anymore."

"The other guys are treating you okay?"

She nodded. "They're tolerating me. Even Blake doesn't growl at me nearly as much as he used to. But I still wish someone would talk to me on occasion. Other than a quick 'Nice play' or 'Good job.'"

"I talk to you."

"You're the only one. And that reminds me. I've been meaning to ask you why."

He looked straight at her and cocked his head slightly to the side, as if to say, "What do you mean?"

"Your attitude toward me has been different than the other boys. Right from the start. Why?"

He smiled. "What time is it?"

She checked her phone, then told him. It was 5:30 pm.

"Do you have a couple minutes?" he asked. "If you do, I'll show you."

She had nothing better to do, so they hopped in his car, which was a black Chevrolet Camaro. It was an older model, but it was in great shape for its age, and he had clearly put some time and effort into it over the years. It had sparkling wheels and a booming stereo, with a huge subwoofer in the trunk.

"You like Green Day?" he asked as he hit a button on the dash.

Brooke nodded. For an older band, Green Day was one of her favorites.

They listened to a song as he drove them to a nearby softball field. A Little League team was practicing. Ten-year-old girls ran everywhere, in a somewhat random fashion, as a pair of coaches tried to instill some sense of order. Brooke instantly had flashbacks to her days as a Little League player, when she played for North Seattle. Those were good days. Things were fun and simple then.

After bringing the car to a stop in the parking lot next to the field, Jamie pointed to one girl, an adorable shortstop with a long, black ponytail and dimples on both cheeks. Brooke was immediately impressed as the girl grabbed a grounder and whipped it to first like she had done it a million times.

"That's my sister," Jamie said. "Her name's Katherine. Everyone calls her Kat for short."

Brooke smiled. "How old is she?"

"She's ten. And as you can see she's a shortstop like you. The minute I saw you, that day Coach West brought you to the field to introduce you to us, I thought of her. She's not as good as you of course, but give her a couple years and she's going to be the star at Silver Lake. I guarantee it."

"Are you close?"

"We have our moments. And a few punches have been thrown over the years. But overall we get along pretty well. We practice in the driveway whenever the weather is good. She's got a great arm for a ten-year-old."

Brooke couldn't help but be touched, and a little jealous. She was an only child, and she had always wanted an older brother who would take care of her and show her the ropes. She hoped Kat realized how good she had it.

"I used to be a shortstop myself," Jamie continued. "But since the team had Dwayne, Coach West moved me to second. When Dwayne got kicked off the team, I thought he was going to move me back, well, at least until you came along."

Brooke instantly grew alarmed. Was Jamie upset she had taken his position?

Clearly he saw the panic in her eyes. He laughed, then said, "Don't worry. It's no big deal. I like playing second and I really just want what's best for the team. Winning conference titles like we did last year is great fun, and if this is what it takes to do it again, so be it."

Brooke was relieved. So far, Jamie was her only ally on the team. She didn't want to risk losing him.

"And I'm kind of hoping you do well. If you can prove girls can play baseball, who knows what doors will open for girls like Kat in the future. Not to say there's anything wrong with playing softball, because there isn't, but it would be nice if girls could do whatever they wanted, right? They could play either sport, softball or baseball?"

Brooke was in shock. Most boys her age spent their time talking about sports, cars, and video games, and they were roughly as intelligent as the common chimp. Her last boyfriend, LeBron Henderson, had been one step above a monkey on the evolutionary scale. She still didn't know what she had seen in him. And her boyfriend before him, Collin Jackson, hadn't been much better. Jamie, on the other hand, seemed completely different. He was contemplative, caring, intelligent, and every other adjective that was synonymous with the word 'good.'

"You up for some ice cream?" he asked.

Like most teenage girls, Brooke was always up for ice cream, especially if it was being purchased for her by a boy. So they drove to the local Cold Stone Creamery, which was in a small strip mall less than a mile away. She ordered her favorite, a double scoop of chocolate ice cream in a waffle cone with caramel, sprinkles, gummy bears, and whipped cream on top. She was really hungry since she hadn't eaten since lunch, so the minute she sat down at a table, she dug in with a passion.

Jamie sat down in the seat across from her. "Wow. You'll fit in with the guys no problem. You eat just like them."

At the sound of his voice, she looked up from her food and stopped abruptly. She had been so hungry she hadn't even realized what she was doing. Much to her chagrin, she had been eating like a pig in front of a boy. How embarrassing.

"I'm just kidding," he said. "But you have something right here."

He reached forward and wiped a small splotch of whipped cream from her chin. She couldn't help but notice how soft his fingers felt as they touched her skin. She instantly started to blush.

It was obvious he saw her cheeks change color, because he smiled, but he didn't say anything more and instead asked her about herself, and she gave him a quick rundown of her life, including how she'd originally been from San Diego, but her family had moved to Seattle when her dad's firm transferred him to its Northwest office. That was a long time ago, when she was just five. She had lived in Seattle since, and her main focus over the years had been softball. She had played Little League until she was eight, then switched to a select team called the Bellevue Beast. She played for the Beast for a couple years, then switched to her current team, the Eastside Angels.

"That's pretty impressive," Jamie said. "I didn't think most girls made a Gold team until they were seniors. And you're a starter, right?"

Brooke nodded. During tryouts, she had beaten out two other girls, both older than her, for the starting position. She downplayed that fact a little, though, because she didn't want Jamie to think she was bragging.

"You don't have to be modest with me. I'm a guy, right? That's what guys do. We go around bragging about ourselves all the time. You should hear Blake when he gets started."

Blake. Brooke cringed the minute Jamie said his name. She hoped he and Jamie weren't too close. She hated the idea of Jamie being friends with a creep like that. And she hoped Jamie didn't know anything about the incident with the jockstrap.

"What's the deal with him?"

"I've known him forever. He's a really nice guy once you get to know him."

"Blake? Are we talking about the same Blake? The overgrown orangutan who plays first base for our team?"

Jamie laughed. "That's actually a pretty good description. But give him a chance and you'll see. He's fiercely loyal once he warms up to you. I remember this one time when we were in middle school, these older kids started picking on me. Blake came along and beat them up. Both of them, at the same time. When I asked him about it, all he said was, 'No one treats my friend like that.' He even got suspended from school for a week for doing it, but he didn't care. He said he had no regrets and he would never let anyone pick on his friend no matter what the consequences were."

Brooke raised an eyebrow. She could hardly believe Blake had any redeeming qualities at all. To her, he was nothing more than a bully.

"What about the other guys?"

"They're all pretty cool. Most of us have been playing together since Little League. We even won state one year. Skinny hit a grand slam in the championship game and I was on third base at the time. It was the most exciting day of my life, at least so far."

The conversation continued from there, and it was a good one. Brooke couldn't believe how many things she and Jamie had in common. Their favorite color was green, they were both Scorpios (her birthday was October 24 and his October 28), they both loved Thai food, they both had been to France (she had gone on a family vacation when she was seven, he had gone when he was ten), and they both loved rock music, the louder the better. Their only major difference was their favorite football teams.

"The Chargers?" he asked. "What's up with that?"

"I'm originally from San Diego, so I've always liked them. And they have cool uniforms. I like the lightning bolts on the helmets. What about you? What's your favorite team?"

"The Seahawks."

"I should have known. Everyone in Seattle loves the Seahawks."

"What's not to love?"

They laughed.

It was at that point Brooke stopped for a second to think about Jamie. As far as she was concerned, he was perfect in every way. He was intelligent, warm, funny, and undeniably cute. She hadn't really noticed it before, but he was. He definitely wasn't a match for Alex, no one was, but he was cute nonetheless, and in a completely different way. He was much more rugged, much less polished, with deep, black hair and auburn eyes. And, to be perfectly honest, his body was dreamy. He wasn't too tall, but he was athletic and muscular, with large biceps, a thick neck, and burly shoulders.

They talked for a while longer, but unfortunately for her, the night had to come to an end sooner or later, so he drove her back to her car at the school parking lot, and she drove herself home from there.

What a fun evening, she thought. *I wish they were all like it.*

Unfortunately, it didn't stay fun for long. Her dad was waiting for her at the door the minute she pulled into the driveway. His face was red and his hair was ruffled.

"Where have you been all night, young lady? I've been worried sick."

Brooke cringed. Normally, her dad called her 'kid,' 'kiddo,' or 'Brooke.' But when she was in trouble she was referred to as 'young lady.'

"Sorry, dad. I lost track of the time."

"I've been texting you all night. Why didn't you respond?"

She cringed. "I left my phone in the car and forgot about it."

He raised a suspicious eyebrow. "A teenage girl forgot about her phone? For over two hours? I find that pretty hard to believe."

Her eyes widened. Had she really been with Jamie for over two hours? To her, it had seemed like fifteen minutes.

"Where were you? I was freaking out. I was about to call the police."

"I went with Jamie to get some ice cream. We were at Cold Stone the whole time."

"Jamie? Do I know her? Is she the new girl on the Angels? The outfielder with the long, brown hair?"

Brooke smiled. Her dad had always had trouble with names. He could never keep her teammates straight. "No, dad, that's Danielle. Jamie is on my baseball team. He's the second baseman."

"He?"

Brooke sighed the minute he said it. A whole new can of worms had just been opened.

Her dad crossed his arms. "Have I met this boy before?"

"You haven't met any of the boys on my team, dad. But you've seen him. At my games."

"Seen him? That's not good enough. No boy is going on a date with my daughter until I meet him first. What if he's a psycho or a loony or something?"

Brooke nearly burst out laughing. Her dad could be so ridiculous at times. "First of all, tonight wasn't a date. We just went to ice cream after practice. And he's not a psycho, or a loony, or anything like that. He's a nice kid. He even has a sister who plays Little League. She's a shortstop like me."

His tone changed immediately. He had a soft spot for shortstops. "Really?"

Brooke nodded. Her dad seemed to soften for a second but then got all rigid and strict again.

"I don't care, young lady. If you want to go out with this Jamie again, so be it, that's your choice, especially if he's a nice kid like you say, but I want to meet him first."

Brooke sighed. "Whatever." She headed inside and trudged upstairs to her bedroom, shaking her head as she went. Her dad could be so stubborn and set in his ways at times. If you looked up the word 'frustrating' in the dictionary, it had a picture of him right next to it.

Chapter 13

They had two games the following week, one against Mountlake Terrace and another against Edmonds-Woodway. Brooke didn't get any hits against Mountlake Terrace, but she made up for it against Edmonds. In the third inning, she got a nice single, straight up the middle, and in the sixth inning she hit a massive shot all the way to deep left field. The ball hit the warning track, took a large bounce, and ended up on the other side of the outfield fence for a ground rule double.

Everyone cheered as she coasted into second. It was her first double as a baseball player, and also her first multi-hit day. As a result, she was nothing but smiles.

But something unexpected happened later in the game. They were ahead 5-0, and there were two outs in the final inning when Edmonds' shortstop hit a sharp grounder at Jamie at second. It was the type of play Jamie normally made with ease, but the ball took a funny hop and jumped over his mitt for an error.

"Come on, Jamie," Alex shouted from his position on the mound. "Get in front of the ball. You know better." He slapped his glove against his thigh and turned back to home plate.

Brooke raised not one, but both of her eyebrows. She had never seen Alex so animated before. Nor so negative. Normally, he was one of the quietest boys on the team, and when he did speak, he was always upbeat and positive. Several of the players on the team had made errors in the past (including her), and he had never said a word about it. He would just take the ball and move on, like all good pitchers did. As such, his reaction toward Jamie was really unexpected and extremely out of character.

But then again, everyone had bad days, and maybe this was one of them. Even the cutest boy in school was allowed to have a bad day or two on occasion, right?

Luckily, he struck out the next batter, ending the game, so no harm was done. A few minutes later, after they shook hands with the other team, Coach West rounded them up for their traditional post-game discussion in center field.

"Well done, guys. And lady. Coaches aren't supposed to give too much praise for fear their players will get cocky and let up, but I'm going to be honest with you. You really look sharp this year. We've won all four games, and we've done it with a combination of good pitching, solid defense, and timely hitting. I'm truly impressed. If we keep working hard, like we've been doing, I'm positive this will be one of the best teams in the school's history."

Brooke liked the sound of that. Wouldn't it be something if the greatest team in the history of the school also just happened to be the first one to have a girl on it?

Coach West made a few more comments and dismissed them, and she rounded up her things and walked to her car in the parking lot. She hoped Jamie would be there to greet her, like he had done the Friday before, and even looked around for him for a couple minutes, but, unfortunately, he and his Camaro were nowhere to be seen.

Chapter 14

Every Tuesday night, Brooke had hitting lessons. Her hitting instructor's name was Steve Johns and he was a really nice guy. He gave lessons in a large industrial complex in south Seattle. It was quite a drive from Brooke's house, especially on a weekday in traffic, but her dad insisted on using Steve because he worked with most of the great softball and baseball players from the area. When they arrived in south Seattle, Steve was finishing up with another girl. He said goodbye to her, then came over and greeted Brooke and her dad in his customary, jovial way.

"How is everything for Miss Brooke this week?"

"Good," she said.

"Sweet. Are you ready to get started?"

She nodded and they began. Her hitting lesson that night consisted of two different stages. The first was called vision training. Brooke stood in a batting cage, in the batter's box, as a machine shot tennis balls at her, one at a time. Each ball was marked with a number, written in one of three colors: red, green, or black. As the ball came at her, she had to hit it, and as she hit it, she had to call out the number and color on the ball. Steve started the machine at a relatively slow speed (fifty miles per hour), then gradually cranked it up to about one hundred miles per hour. At that speed, the ball was little more than a yellow blur, but Brooke had been doing the drill for long enough she could usually see the colors on the ball, and sometimes the numbers, regardless of the speed. The process helped improve her focus and concentration, and it took about half an hour.

After she finished her vision training, they moved to another batting cage and Steve tossed her balls from behind a protective screen. He watched her form as she hit each toss and stopped her periodically to correct little flaws in her swing. They hadn't even completed the first bucket of balls when Brooke's dad brought the drill to a quick and premature end.

"What are you doing, Brooke?" Like always, he stood outside the cage watching everything attentively.

Brooke turned to him with a blank look on her face. She had no idea what he was talking about. She was doing everything exactly the same way she always had.

"I thought you were serious about playing baseball," he said.

"I am."

"Then show it. Put the softballs away and get the baseballs out."

There was complete confusion in Steve's eyes. "Baseballs?"

They explained to him that Brooke had joined the school's baseball team and his eyes got big with excitement the minute he heard the news.

"You've already played four games? Well done, Miss Brooke. Why didn't you tell me about this sooner? How are you hitting?"

"Pretty well. I have four hits so far. One was a ground-rule double."

"And she nearly had another," her dad said, "but the outfielder made a good running catch. But she could do better. She's dropping her hands again. Not much, but enough to make a difference, so you need to work on it."

So they did. With a zeal. Steve exchanged the bucket of softballs for a bucket of baseballs and they went to town. It was great fun, the most fun they had had for a while, and they worked for at least twice as long as normal. Brooke couldn't help but notice how even the smallest change, like just changing the type of the balls she was using, could get everyone so excited. Even her dad, who had been so dead-set against her playing baseball at first, was nothing but smiles as she lined a pitch straight up the middle that missed Steve by less than an inch.

"Darn, Miss Brooke," Steve said. "You're dangerous as a baseball player."

"You bet I am," she said with a laugh.

Chapter 15

Their next game was against Kamiak. Like most of their games, it was well played by both teams, but in the end Kamiak's pitcher was simply no match for Alex. As a result, Silver Lake won 3-0, and they did so pretty easily. Blake hit a home run, Skinny got two doubles, Jamie got two singles, and Brooke added one. Everyone was stellar in the field and Kamiak never got a runner past second.

But the second game of the week, the one against Glacier Peak, was the one Brooke would remember forever. Alex was absolutely on fire, even better than normal. His fastball was untouchable, as was his curveball, off-speed, and splitter. The Glacier Peak hitters were absolutely overwhelmed. By the sixth inning, Silver Lake was leading 6-0 and all of its players, including Brooke, were excited. But they weren't excited about the score.

They were excited about the no-hitter.

A no-hitter is the holy grail of baseball. It is when a pitcher pitches an entire game and never gives up a single hit. It is rarely done by anyone at any level.

Alex was pitching a no-hitter.

Even he was excited. Even though he had pitched all his life, he had never thrown a no-hitter. Twice he had gotten close and had thrown one-hitters, but an opposing batter had always found a way to spoil his bid for perfection.

The tension was absolutely intense. As they took the field to begin the seventh and final inning, Brooke could feel it. Everyone, the players, the coaches, the fans, they all wanted Alex to get the no-hitter.

"You can do it, son," Alex's dad called from the stands. "Focus. Three more outs."

That was the first time Brooke had ever seen Alex's dad, and she immediately understood why Alex was so good looking. His dad, for a man his age, was incredible. He was tall and lean, with sharp features and a strong, chiseled jaw. His hair had begun to gray, but it in no way detracted from his overall appearance. If anything, it made him look more elegant and more dignified.

Alex was normally the calmest player on the field, but not on that day. He was sweating profusely. Brooke could see it from her position at short. And he was walking all over the mound between pitches. He went from one side to the other, wiped his brow, caught the ball, then walked back to the other side, then over to the other. As good as he was, he clearly wasn't used to being in this type of position with so much at stake.

But he did his job. It took five pitches, but he struck out the first batter to start the inning. Brooke cheered the minute the batter swung at the final pitch. Only two more to go.

The next batter hit a slow grounder to JJ at third. JJ rushed in, grabbed it with his mitt, and tossed it to Blake for out number two.

Brooke was in heaven. There was only one out to go. The no-hitter was so close she could taste it.

But there was a problem. Alex was a wreck. He didn't say anything, but Brooke could see it in his face. His eyes were wide and his cheeks were pale. He wanted this no-hitter so bad he wasn't even breathing.

Amazingly, however, that wasn't their biggest problem. Their biggest problem was Glacier Peak's next batter. He was a big kid named Jessie Johnson, a power hitting lefty, who was built like a bodybuilder. He was so big his muscles had muscles. Alex had gotten him out during his first two at-bats, but it hadn't been easy either time. Jessie's first shot had been a monster fly to center that Terrell had caught on the run, and his second shot had been a laser that Blake had snared at the last second, saving at least a double.

And the no-hitter. Had that ball gotten by Blake, Alex's beloved no-hitter would have been history.

Brooke crouched down at short. She needed to be ready. If Jessie got a hold of one of Alex's pitches, it wasn't going to be pretty.

And it wasn't. Just as she had worried, Jessie hit one of Alex's pitches, the very first one, and he hit it well, a line drive about five feet high straight up the middle. At first Brooke thought she had no chance at it, since Jessie had hit it so sharply, but she got a good jump on it and raced directly for it as fast as she could. The ball had made it to second, and even at the speed she was going she would never have been able to get to it unless she did something drastic. So she did. She dove. Like most girls, she had never liked diving since hitting the ground usually hurt, a lot, but she had no choice. And it ended up being the best dive she had ever made, completely outstretched as far as she could go. Even so, she barely got it. The ball stuck in the top of her glove, in the webbing, in what players call an 'ice cream cone.' Almost instantaneously, she came crashing to the ground, knocking the wind from her lungs. It was even more painful than the time she had run into the catcher in the game against Meadowdale. At first she thought the impact of the ground had jarred the ball free and she had dropped it, since she had barely gotten a hold of it in the first place, but then she looked up and saw it was still sitting there, in the very top of her mitt, less than an inch from the ground.

"She's got it," the umpire shouted. "It's a catch. The game is over."

To Brooke, the next fifteen minutes were a complete blur. She still hadn't recovered from hitting the ground so hard, and she still couldn't breathe, but it didn't matter. Alex threw his mitt into the sky and charged to her from his position on the mound. He scooped her up and lifted her high into the air, hugging her tightly against him, spinning her around and around and around. He was so excited he couldn't help himself. After all the years of trying, and after all the failed attempts, he had finally gotten his no-hitter.

"Thank you, thank you, thank you, thank you."

She didn't know how many times he said it, nor did she really care. All she knew was she was being hugged by the cutest boy in the school and she liked it. A lot. A few seconds later, the rest of her teammates arrived, and they tackled the two of them right there on the spot. It was the funnest, but heaviest, pig pile Brooke had ever been in. At one point, Blake's knee was in her back, Skinny's knee was in her chest, and someone else's elbow was crammed against the side of her face, and it was all quite painful, but even so she couldn't stop smiling.

She had made the catch. Somehow, she had done it, and thanks to her, Alex had gotten his no-hitter.

It got even better after the game. Brooke watched as Alex's dad met him at the side of the field and gave him an enormous bear hug. Minutes later, a small truck pulled up, and a news reporter interviewed Alex for the next day's paper. But the absolute highlight happened a few minutes later, and it involved the last person Brooke would have ever expected.

Blake.

He walked up to her out of nowhere, completely by himself. He had already taken his jersey off and was only wearing his Under Armour. His face was a mess, and it looked like he had been crying tears of joy. "I never wanted you on the team, Brooke, and I'm still not certain I do, but I'll be honest. That was the best catch I've ever seen. I don't know how you did it. It was insane."

Without another word, he turned and rushed away, to resume celebrating with Alex and the other boys.

Chapter 16

Brooke's softball team, the Angels, had a tournament the following weekend in a city to the east of Seattle named Redmond. It was a nice place, and Brooke had always liked playing there, but, as she had expected, the focus wasn't on their game.

"Oh my God," Aubrey said, her eyes as big as saucers. The girls had just finished their warmups and were sitting in their dugout, waiting for the day's first game to begin. "Let me get this straight. You were on the ground, rolling around with an entire team of boys, all at the same time? And Alex was one of them?"

Brooke had just finished telling them what had happened during the game against Glacier Peak. About how she had saved Alex's no-hitter with a diving catch. But the girls, especially Aubrey, weren't interested in the no-hitter, nor the diving catch. All they wanted to hear about was Alex hugging her after the game.

"I'd pay money to roll around with Alex on the ground," Aubrey said. "And all you had to do was make a diving catch? I'll make a diving catch. Watch me next inning."

They laughed. Aubrey was quite a riot, especially when she got excited. And she always got excited when she was talking about Alex.

"Here's what I want to know," Faith said. "Even that big guy, the one you said is so mean all the time, even he was impressed?"

Brooke nodded. "He said it was the best catch he's ever seen. I couldn't believe it. I still can't. And the next day at practice, I couldn't really do much since my side was sore from when I hit the ground, so I just sat in the dugout for most of the day. All of a sudden, Blake comes up to me and says, 'Just take it easy today, Brooke. Get some rest and heal up. We need you ready for Monday.'"

The girls looked at her with curious expressions on their faces.

"What's on Monday?" Naomi asked.

"Our next game. And it's a big one. It's against Alderwood."

The girls nodded. They knew Alderwood well. Alderwood and Silver Lake were arch rivals.

"Last year," Brooke said, "we beat them for the league title, but this year, the paper picked them as the favorites. As a result, the guys have been talking about it all season. Their pitcher is a senior named Christian Parkinson. They say he's as good and as nasty as they get. He's got five different pitches, and he throws them all well. They say his control is amazing, as is his velocity. And apparently he's mean, too."

"Mean?" Naomi asked. "What do you mean by that?"

"He's been known to throw brushback pitches for the fun of it."

In unison, the girls groaned. A brushback pitch is a pitch that is high and tight, and it usually misses the batter by mere inches. It is usually done to scare the batter or to get her to move away from the plate. The girls didn't like brushback pitches at all. Especially Brooke, who had been hit by several over the years. She still had a small bump on her left forearm from when a pitcher had hit her and it had never healed quite right.

"Like always," she continued, "we play every team twice this year, so the game on Monday isn't a do-or-die situation, but we want to win anyway to send a message. And it will give us a one game lead in the standings."

"Has Alderwood lost any games so far?" Faith asked.

Brooke shook her head. "Like us, they're undefeated. And none of their games have been close. They beat Meadowdale 10-0 yesterday."

She was about to say something more but was interrupted as one of the assistant coaches called frantically from the far end of the dugout. The game had started, but the girls had been so focused on their conversation they hadn't even noticed. Brooke grabbed her bat and darted for the batter's box.

They were playing a team from West Seattle called West Seattle Fastpitch. WSF's pitcher was a short, stocky girl named Kaitlyn Rogers, and Kaitlyn was a good pitcher, but she was nothing special. Normally, she was no match for Brooke, but Brooke was worried anyway. Now that she had put so much time and effort into baseball, she had little confidence in her softball skills and she wasn't certain she could even hit a softball anymore.

Luckily for her, she could. Kaitlyn got two strikes on her, but then made an error by leaving a change-up over the middle of the plate. To Brooke, who had gotten used to hitting a baseball, the softball looked like a big, fat grapefruit. She kept her hands up, her chin down, and hammered the ball into center field for a single. Two runs scored as a result.

Her dad, who sat in his customary spot in the front row of the bleachers, cheered loudly. "Well done, kid. Way to keep your eyes on the ball. Nice hit."

Brooke could hardly believe it. Despite her terrible start to the season, despite her struggles in both baseball and softball, and despite all of her problems with the boys and her dad, everything was finally falling into place.

Or so she thought.

Things got ugly on Monday.

Chapter 17

They were all excited about the game on Monday afternoon. It was the first game of the season against their arch rivals, a nearby school named Alderwood. No one liked Alderwood because it was a new school, recently built just a few years before, and it was filled with preppy rich kids. All of Alderwood's teams were good, but their baseball team was by far the best of the bunch. Everyone knew that, barring a major upset, the league champion that year would be either Alderwood or Silver Lake.

The game was at Alderwood, and as the Silver Lake bus arrived, the Eagles were warming up on the field. Brooke's eyes got large as she took a look at them for the first time. They were huge, every one of them. They looked more like a football team than a baseball team.

"They don't scare me," Blake said as he marched his way toward the field.

One of Alderwood's players called out to them as Brooke reached the dugout and started to unload her equipment. "So it's true. Mighty Silver Lake has gotten so desperate for players they've turned to the softball team for help."

Blake walked up to him and got in his face. The other boy was big, there was no mistaking that, but he was no match for Blake.

"You got an issue with that?" Blake asked.

The other boy turned and left without a response. They all laughed.

Normally, Brooke would have been offended by the boy's comment, but there was something about it that made her happy.

Blake's reaction. Her greatest nemesis, the boy who had hated her from the start, had stood up for her. And she had no doubt that, had the Alderwood boy pressed the issue further, a fight would have ensued. She had only known Blake for a short time, but she had already learned one thing about him. He didn't back down. Ever.

Brooke grinned as Alderwood took the field to start the game. The pitcher, Christian Parkinson, was the boy Blake had chased away. Unfortunately, Brooke wasn't smiling for long. Christian was everything she had heard. To put it bluntly, he was awesome. He threw even harder than Alex. He struck out all three of their batters in the first inning, and one of three in the second.

Luckily, Alex was up to the challenge. He struck out two batters in the first and two in the second. When Brooke got her first at-bat in the third, there were two outs and the game was still scoreless.

Christian snickered as he watched her step up to the plate. He shook his head in disgust.

"How stupid is this? A girl playing baseball? Don't you have anything better to do? Like paint your nails?"

Brooke didn't know what to say in response, so she said nothing.

"You're a good looking chick, Brooke. I can think of a few things you can do for me. But none of them involve baseball."

The umpire stepped forward. "That's enough, Christian. I'll have no more comments like that. Shut your mouth and play ball."

Christian shrugged. "Fine. Let's see what this little girl has got." His voice was filled with disdain.

It was the fastest fastball Brooke had ever seen. Regardless, she was ready, and she got a piece of it and fouled it away.

Christian was both surprised and a little impressed. He hadn't expected her to have a chance, not for a second.

The next pitch was even faster than the first. Brooke fouled it away, too.

Christian's mood changed in a heartbeat. After the first pitch, he had looked mildly amused. But after the second, he looked angry. He couldn't believe a girl had fought off two of his best pitches.

"You think you're good? Let's see exactly how good you are. And how tough."

The next pitch was a complete blur. Before Brooke could do a thing, it hit her in the side of the head. It hit her so hard it blew her off her feet and knocked her to the ground. She landed in a crumpled heap and her bat bounced to the side. It hurt so bad she thought she was going to die. Tears streamed down her cheeks. The last thing she remembered was the sound of the umpire above her, saying desperately, "Young lady, young lady? Are you okay? Someone call an ambulance. Now."

Less than a second later, she blacked out.

An hour later, she awoke in a hospital bed. The second she regained consciousness, she reached up and grabbed her temples. Her head felt like it was going to explode. A doctor, a nurse, and her dad stood over her.

"Here she comes," the doctor said. He was a small man with dark hair and matching eyes.

"Thank God," her dad said. "How are you, kiddo?"

Brooke was totally disoriented and she didn't know where she was. All she remembered was a bright, white flash, and then overwhelming darkness. She sat up in the hospital bed and tried to get her bearings.

"Take it easy," her dad said. "Not too fast, kid."

The doctor turned to the nurse. "Now that she's conscious, I want a CAT scan, pronto."

Ever so carefully, the nurse moved Brooke into a wheelchair and pushed her down the hall, to another room where they could complete the CAT scan and make certain she didn't have any internal bleeding or other damage to her brain or skull. Along the way, bits and pieces of what had happened came back to her in frightening, violent flashes, and her dad filled her in with the rest of the details.

"You gave us quite a scare. I've never seen a player hit the ground so hard. And you didn't move at all, not an inch, until the paramedics arrived. For a minute . . . ." His words trailed off abruptly. He didn't want to complete the sentence.

It took a long time, but luckily everything went okay with the CAT scan. Apparently, her batting helmet had done its job and had saved her from any serious physical damage. The doctor thought she'd be fine after a few days of rest.

"But I want a follow-up in one week. And no physical activities until then. Especially softball."

"What about baseball?" she asked.

The doctor looked at her with a puzzled expression on his face. He was clearly confused.

"She plays baseball," her dad said. "In addition to softball."

"Really?" the doctor asked. "I didn't know girls played baseball. Sweet. Regardless, no strenuous activity of any type until I say it's okay. That means no sports of any type – softball or baseball."

"But I've got more games this week," Brooke said. "The team needs me."

"And she's got a tournament this weekend," her dad added.

The doctor was resolute. "Absolutely not. We can't take any chances with this type of thing. Everything looks okay now, but you never know. I've seen cases where the initial scans come back okay, then everything goes downhill from there. If everything looks okay after a week, I'll clear you and then you can return to play. But not until then. Understood?"

Brooke and her dad were not happy, not at all, but they had no choice but to agree. Like always, the doctor knew best, and they both knew that there were few things that were more dangerous to a person's wellbeing than a head injury.

"And Brooke," the doctor said. "Before you leave, we're going to need a urine sample."

Brooke cringed. Peeing into a cup was not one of her favorite activities, not at all. But at least it was good timing. She had to go. And she had to go bad.

Something nice happened before they left the hospital. Jamie showed up. He was still in his baseball uniform and had come straight from the game. There was a look of exhaustion and concern in his eyes.

"Are you okay? I got here as fast as I could."

"I've got a nasty headache, and the doctor says my dad has to wake me up every two hours tonight to make certain I don't slip into a coma, but other than that I should be fine." She then thought of something. "How did the game go? Did we win?"

Jamie shook his head. "We lost."

Brooke sighed. Her day had just gone from bad to worse. After all she'd been through, she'd hoped to hear the team had won. At least that would have made her feel a little better.

"What happened?"

"It got really ugly after you blacked out. Blake nearly tore Christian's head off. He got a hold of him and pinned him to the ground right there on the field. It took all of us to pull him away."

Brooke could hardly believe what she had just heard.

"Blake? Blake attacked Christian?"

"I already told you, he's fiercely loyal once you win him over. And apparently you won him over. So he was going to make Christian pay for what he had done."

Brooke was speechless.

"But things got even worse. Christian was Alderwood's first batter the next inning. Alex hit him in the head with the very first pitch. I couldn't believe it. I've never seen him hit a batter before. Not on purpose."

Brooke's mouth dropped open. She was flabbergasted.

"They had to call another ambulance, this one for Christian. The umpire threw Alex out of the game, claiming he did it on purpose, which he clearly did. Coach West got in a huge argument with the umpire, and he got thrown out, too. He claimed the umpire was at fault, since he should have thrown Christian out for hitting you. But he wouldn't leave until they called the cops. In the meantime, he threw all kinds of stuff onto the field, just like managers do in those videos you see on YouTube. That part was actually pretty cool. But anyway, I pitched the rest of the game and I did the best I could, but it's been a long time since I last pitched. We got one run, thanks to JJ, but they got two in the bottom of the sixth and we couldn't come back. After all that had happened, we were out of gas. And it was so hard to concentrate after you left. Everyone was worried sick. We got your dad's number from someone in the stands and called him for an update, but at that point he didn't have anything to tell us. He said you were still unconscious."

She didn't know what to say. Her mind was on overdrive, trying to process all the information she'd just been told, but with her headache it wasn't an easy task. She couldn't believe it. Blake had started a fight, Alex had gotten himself thrown out of the game, and Coach West had gone crazy. All for her.

Now she knew. Despite being a girl, they had fully accepted her. They wouldn't have acted the way they had or done the things they had done unless they considered her a legitimate member of the team.

Despite the constant pounding in her head, she felt good.

Chapter 18

The ensuing week was tough for Brooke. It took two full days for her headache to go away, and even after it went away, she still had trouble sleeping. She kept having nightmares of Christian. He was standing on the mound, with the ball in his hand and a twisted, menacing look on his face.

"You think you're good?" he said. "Let's see how good you are."

She'd jolt awake the instant the ball hit her, and she'd be covered in sweat every time.

But her dreams weren't her only problem. Her dad got finicky again. It happened on Wednesday night, right after he got home from work. She was watching television in the living room, with a maple bar in one hand and her phone in the other, when he plopped down on the couch next to her.

"I've been thinking about this baseball thing again. Maybe it's not a good idea after all."

"What?" Brooke asked. She couldn't believe it. "You said you'd support me. We already talked about this."

"I know. But that was before you got injured."

"I've been injured before, dad. I get injured all the time. Remember that time a few years back during practice when Naomi slid into my foot and broke my toenail off? That was bad. I could barely walk for a week. And what about that time at McCall Field when the ball hit third base and shot up into my face, and I would have lost all of my front teeth if it wasn't for my braces?"

Her dad nodded. "I remember it well. It isn't a fond memory."

"And what about that time in Little League, when I slid back into third base and I jammed my wrist so bad it turned purple?"

He smiled. "I still can't believe you finished that game."

"I had to bat with one hand. It hurt too much to use the other one. And what about the time the ball hit my thumb and it swelled up so bad you had to leave work early to take me for x-rays?"

"I thought it was broken for sure."

"Me, too. Anyway, it doesn't matter what sport I'm playing, softball or baseball, I can still get injured and I probably will. I always get injured. What do you call me?"

"Accident prone?"

"No, not that one. The other one."

"A ball magnet?"

"Yeah, that's it. I just have bad luck. No matter where I go, the ball finds me and hits me. It's just a matter of when and where."

He couldn't deny it, since it was true. But there was one distinction.

"In softball, a pitcher never threw at your head before."

"That Christian is a bad apple. But it doesn't mean all boys are like him. I've played in several games so far this season, and he's the only one who's done it."

"You've still got to play him again, later in the season. What if he does it again?"

A lump formed in Brooke's throat and her eyes got big. She hadn't thought of that, and she didn't like it at all.

"I hate those Alderwood kids," her dad said. "They're a bunch of spoiled brats. I should get someone to burn that school down. That would do us all a favor."

Brooke smiled. Burning the school down did seem like a pretty good solution.

"But then again," her dad said, "I'd go to prison for twenty years, and I'd miss your games, and I wouldn't like that at all."

"I've been meaning to ask you about that. Why did you come to my baseball games? You were so against it. I was certain you wouldn't come."

"I only have a few games left. I need to enjoy them while I can."

Brooke was puzzled by his words. "What do you mean?"

"How old are you?"

Brooke rolled her eyes. Her dad could never remember how old she was.

"Sixteen."

"Oh yeah. Well then you've only got two years left until you graduate, and then you'll be done playing, and I won't have any games left to watch. So I've got to watch as many as I can now."

"But I'm going to play in college."

"I know, but you're probably going to be at some school in California, and I'll fly down there when I can, but it's not going to be the same."

Brooke smiled. Her dad was so funny. Like all guys, he liked to spend the majority of his day walking around acting all machismo, but at the same time there was a sentimental side to him, too. And he had always been really overprotective of her, but that was partially her own fault. She had always been a 'daddy's girl' and she still remembered the time when she was three and she flipped her tricycle and scraped her arm. Her mom had only been a few feet away from her when it happened, but she ran right past her to get to her dad so he could make it better. Not to say she wasn't close with her mom, because she was, but in a different way. Her dad had been the one to teach her how to ride her bike, and to drive, and most importantly, to play softball.

And softball had always been their closest bond. Her dad had taught her how to play as soon as she could walk. They'd be out in the back yard for hours, with a little plastic bat, hitting until the sun went down. Even in the winter months, when it got dark before her dad got home from work, they'd still practice. They went to a local hardware store and got some porch lights that lit up the majority of the yard. Brooke remembered some days it was so cold she could see her breath and barely feel her fingers, but it never stopped them, not once. They even played one day in the snow, but their practice came to a premature end when she hit the ball too hard and it flew over the fence and the neighbor's dog, Rascal, ran off with it.

Her dad interrupted her thoughts.

"What's the name of that boy who came to the hospital?"

"What? What boy?"

"When you got hurt. That boy at the hospital. I saw him when I was returning from the parking lot."

"That was Jamie. The second baseman. He's the boy I went to ice cream with that one night. When you got mad at me for not answering your calls."

"I like him."

Brooke nearly fell off the couch. Her dad had never liked any of the boys she had introduced him to. He had that typical 'no boy is good enough for my daughter' attitude you found in a lot of dads.

"What do you mean?"

"That was nice of him, to come and see you and all. Since you're new on the team, he barely knows you, but he came anyway. That's the type of boy you should be dating. Not that Spyder boy. I hate that kid."

Brooke nearly burst out laughing. The 'Spyder boy' he had referred to was Bobby Sullivan, her boyfriend in the eighth grade. Everyone called him Spyder because he had a pet tarantula.

"Dad, I already told you I didn't know he was a smoker until after I started seeing him. And as soon as I found out, I broke up with him."

"What about that Hugh kid?"

Brooke cringed. Hugh was her boyfriend in the ninth grade. He had been a total creep. She had no idea what she had seen in him.

"You have terrible taste in boys."

"Oh my God." She couldn't believe what she had just heard. Her dad was critiquing her choice of boyfriends. Somewhat sarcastically, she said, "Would you like to pick my next boyfriend?"

"Actually, I would."

Now she had heard everything. "Do you know how ridiculous that sounds?"

He chuckled. "You're probably right. But if I could, I'd pick that Jamie kid. He seems like a nice kid to me. That's the type of boy you should be seeing."

Brooke didn't say anything, but she had no choice but to agree. Jamie was definitely the nicest boy she had met since joining the baseball team. As far as she could tell, he was perfect in every way.

Her dad changed the subject. "How are you feeling today?"

"Okay."

"Headache any better?"

"A little." Actually, it was pretty much gone, but she didn't want to tell him quite yet. She had always liked sympathy, and her headache had gotten her a lot of it.

"Good. Hopefully you'll get better soon. It would be nice to see you on the field again."

Brooke looked at him with a blank look on her face. How inconsistent was that? Five minutes before, he had wanted her to quit the team. Now, he wanted her to play again?

"What do you mean?"

"I actually like this baseball thing. The other night at your batting lesson with Steve, that was the most fun I've had in awhile. And that catch you made to save the no-hitter. That was incredible. I've been bragging about it at the office all week. How many guys can say they have a daughter who is so talented she can compete with boys? Some of my partners are so impressed they're going to come and watch one of your upcoming games."

"Really? Sweet."

"I thought so, too. So do us a favor and get better quick."

With a smile, he hopped up and headed upstairs to change out of his suit.

Chapter 19

The remaining games that week were agonizing for Brooke. She was what some coaches call a workhorse — the type of player who likes to play every inning of every game. She hated sitting on the bench watching. And she especially hated it now that she had finally proven herself to the boys. Now that she fit in, she wanted to be out there with them, contributing as much as possible.

But she wasn't going to be cleared until the following Monday, so she had no choice but to sit and watch.

The game on Tuesday, their second game of the season against Edmonds-Woodway, went well. Silver Lake's athletic director suspended Alex and Coach West one game each for their roles in the Alderwood game, so neither of them were allowed to participate. Neither of them were even allowed to be there. An assistant coach took Coach West's place and Jamie did the pitching. And he did a good job. He only gave up four hits and they won 3-1. Blake hit a two-run homer and Terrell added a solo shot. The only down spot was Brooke's replacement, Benji Hampton. Benji was a freshman and the normal starter on the JV team, but they called him up to fill in for Brooke until she could return. He struck out all three at-bats and made two errors in the field. The second was on a throw from Skinny behind the plate. Skinny's throw was great, and absolute laser that would have nailed the runner by a mile, but Benji dropped it.

When the inning was over, Skinny walked up to Brooke in the dugout. She was sitting on the bench doing little more than twiddling her thumbs.

"I hope the doctor clears you soon, Brooke. I can't take much more of Benji."

On Thursday, for their game against Meadowdale, Alex and Coach West were back and they cruised to another easy victory. Jamie led the way with three singles and Blake had another home run, a massive shot to center. It was the longest home run Brooke had ever seen, and it ended up in the middle of a large pond. The highlight of the game, however, came at the end of the fourth inning. Alex walked into the dugout, tossed his mitt to the side, and sat down right next to Brooke.

"How are you?"

She nearly passed out on the spot. It was the first time he had ever spoken to her. Other than the time she had saved his no-hitter, but even then, all he had said was "Thank you."

She straightened her bangs as quickly as she could. "Okay."

"I never got a chance to really thank you for that catch. I know most shortstops wouldn't have even tried for that ball. I'll never forget what you did."

She could feel her cheeks getting warm. Oh God, was she blushing? How embarrassing.

"My dad already got a stand for the ball," he continued. "With one of those fancy customized bases, and he put it in my trophy room. I've been treated like royalty ever since."

He turned to face her, and her heart raced the minute he did it. He was even cuter close-up than he was from afar. His deep blue eyes were absolutely radiant as he spoke.

"I owe you. If you ever need anything, anything at all, just ask and it's yours."

Coach West called out to him, so without another word he hopped up and got ready for his next at-bat. The minute he walked away, Brooke grabbed her phone. She had to text Aubrey and tell her what had happened. Unfortunately, one of the assistant coaches saw what she was doing and frowned.

"I don't know about softball players, but baseball players don't text in the dugout."

Brooke was unfazed. She waited until he wasn't looking, then continued her message. This information was way too important to wait.

"You won't believe it," she wrote. "Alex just sat down next to me and talked to me. He said he'll never forget my catch. He says he owes me."

Aubrey's response was instant. "OMG. You're the luckiest girl in the world."

Chapter 20

The doctor cleared Brooke on Monday, and her first game was the next day against Mountlake Terrace. Unfortunately, returning to play wasn't as easy as she had hoped. She was jumpy. She was afraid the ball was going to hit her again, and during her first at-bat she jumped away from the plate even though the pitch wasn't anywhere near her. She struck out her first two at-bats before getting a bloop single in the bottom of the sixth. It was just over the third baseman's hands and was more luck than anything, but at that point she was willing to take anything she could get. In the field, she was solid, and she caught a throw from Skinny and slapped it on the runner's foot just before he touched second base.

"Out!" the umpire yelled.

Skinny trotted up to her as the inning ended. "It's nice to have you back. Do me a favor and don't get hurt again."

They won the game easily, beating Mountlake Terrace 6-2. Jamie got two singles and a double, and Blake had a triple. As always, Alex was stellar on the mound. He finished the game with ten strikeouts.

Their next game was against Glacier Peak and once again they cruised. Brooke still felt a little uneasy at the plate, but she gained some new confidence and inspiration when she looked in the stands and saw her dad and two other men who were both wearing fancy suits. No doubt they were his partners from his law office. They cheered as she got a single in the second inning and laid down a perfect sacrifice bunt, right down the third base foul line, in the fourth. The loudest cheer, however, came in the fifth inning, when she, Jamie, and Blake turned a double play to end the inning.

"That's my girl," her dad called. "Perfect throw, kid."

The highlight of the game, however, came the next inning, in the dugout. Alex was sitting on the bench with an open space next to him, and, after a few seconds of contemplation, Brooke managed to build up the courage to sit down right next to him.

"You guys are making my job pretty easy," he said.

"Excuse me?" she said.

"It's pretty easy to be a pitcher when you have a great defense behind you. And you guys are a great defense. That double play was sweet."

"Thanks."

They sat there for a second before she got the courage to say something more. There was something she had been wondering about and had wanted to ask Alex about for a while.

"Do you mind if I ask you something?"

He turned to her and smiled. "Fire away."

"That day when Christian hit me with the pitch, did you hit him on purpose? Jamie said you did."

His only response was a nod.

"Why?" she asked.

"No one hits my shortstop and gets away with it. Especially if that shortstop is you."

It was his turn to bat, so he didn't get a chance to elaborate any further. Regardless, it didn't matter to Brooke. She was happy anyway. The fact he had referred to her as 'his shortstop' was more than enough for her. It was the best compliment she could have ever received. She grabbed her phone.

"OMG," Aubrey wrote back. "Then what did he say?"

"He said, 'Especially if that shortstop is you.'"

"OMG. He likes you. There's no doubt about it. No doubt at all."

"No way."

"WAY!"

That night, as Brooke climbed into her bed, she kept repeating Alex's words over and over in her mind. She was absolutely obsessed with what he had said.

"No one hits my shortstop and gets away with it. Especially if that shortstop is you."

The first sentence was the one that had originally gotten her attention, but it was the second sentence that now had her so fixated.

"Especially if that shortstop is you."

What did it mean? Aubrey was convinced it was Alex's way of telling Brooke he liked her. But even if that were true, how exactly did he like her? Did he 'like' like her, as in how friends like one another, or 'really' like her, as in boyfriend-girlfriend type of stuff? And if it was the boyfriend-girlfriend type of stuff, how could that be, since he already had a girlfriend, Alyssa?

Needless to say, Brooke tossed and turned all night, and she didn't actually get to sleep until around 3:00 am.

Chapter 21

The next day, life got even better. It was Friday, so like every Friday, everyone was excited for the weekend and a couple days off. Brooke sat at a table in the school cafeteria eating lunch with Naomi, Faith, and Aubrey. Aubrey was in the middle of giving them the latest gossip when her eyes got big and she stopped mid-sentence. That was incredibly strange since Aubrey rarely, if ever, stopped talking, and she never did so in the middle of a sentence. In addition, the color had drained completely from her face. Brooke turned to see what she was looking at and realized Alex was standing right behind her. Like always, he looked amazing, and he was wearing a black jacket, gray T-shirt, and faded jeans.

"Hi, Brooke. I wanted to stop by and see how you're doing today."

Brooke felt like the queen of the world. The cutest boy at the school had stopped by her table to see how she was doing. She could barely contain her excitement. "Good. I'm good. How about you?"

"I'm good. But then again, life is always good on Fridays, right? Anyway, my parents are out of town this weekend, at their place in Palm Springs, so I was going to have a party tonight, so feel free to come by if you'd like. The whole team will be there. And feel free to bring anyone you want, so if the rest of you ladies would like to come, that'd be great. I've heard a lot of good things about the softball team this year so it would be nice to spend a little time with you."

Brooke was flabbergasted. "Party? At your place? Tonight?"

"Yeah. But if you do come do me a favor and bring some chips or other goodies. Whatever you like. I'll get a bunch of stuff, too, but you can never have too much, especially when Blake and Skinny are around. Those are some big boys and trust me, they eat like it."

"Chips. I can bring chips."

His eyes got big. "So that means you'll come?"

Brooke nodded so hard she almost gave herself whiplash.

"Sweet. You totally made my day. What about the rest of you?" He looked around at the other girls.

"Yes," they all blurted, in unison.

He smiled. "Sweet. I can't wait to see you all there. Let's plan on meeting at 8:00."

The minute he left, Aubrey started to hyperventilate. "Oh my God. Did that really happen? Did it? Someone pinch me. I think I'm dreaming. No, wait. Don't pinch me. If this is a dream, I don't want to wake up, ever."

Naomi's eyes were almost as large as Aubrey's. "I can't believe it. We just got invited to a party at Alex Anderson's house. I never thought I'd see the day. It's amazing."

"No it's not," Faith said. "It's not that big a deal."

Unlike the rest of the girls, she didn't seem impressed.

"It isn't?" Naomi asked.

"No."

"So you're not going?"

"Of course I'm going. I wouldn't miss it for all the money in the world. But even so, it's still not that big a deal."

They all laughed. Faith could be so ridiculous at times.

Alex's party was all Brooke could think about the rest of the day. In math class, they had a pop quiz, and she couldn't concentrate so she bombed it miserably, but it didn't matter, not in the least. All that mattered was the fact she was going to Alex's party that night. In the meantime, however, she had a lot to do. She had to pick out something to wear, do her hair, get some breath mints, etc. And she barely managed to get ready in time. The girls picked her up at 7:30 pm and they rode together in Faith's car to Alex's house. His dad was some type of big-time real estate developer and they lived in a ritzy part of town in the fanciest house Brooke had ever seen. It was more like a mansion than a house. It had a long driveway in the front, lined with tall, perfectly manicured hedges, a swimming pool with a waterfall in the back, and a gorgeous view of the Cascade mountains to one side.

Alex greeted them the minute they rang the doorbell. Already, a lot of kids were there, mostly seniors, but some juniors and sophomores. The place was packed and people milled about in just about every room imaginable, and there were a lot of rooms. Most of the baseball team was there, but Brooke hardly recognized them, since she had rarely seen them without their uniforms or practice gear. Terrell, Skinny, and Blake sat in the living room playing a video game on the largest television Brooke had ever seen.

They looked up the minute the girls walked into the room. Blake motioned to Terrell.

"Show some manners, schmuck. Give Brooke your chair."

Terrell shook his head, clearly disgusted. "Let me guess. Since she's a lady, she gets my chair?"

"No," Blake said. "Since she's an infielder, she gets your chair. We infielders stick together."

Terrell shook his head, but he did as told. Somewhat hesitantly, and not knowing what else to do, Brooke took his seat.

"You any good at video games?" Blake asked.

"Not really." To be perfectly honest, Brooke had never really liked video games too much. Except Rock Band. But she wasn't going to tell Blake that.

"This is my favorite fighting game," he said. "Here, I'll teach you."

He handed her a controller and showed her how to play, and she spent the next ten minutes doing her best. And it was actually pretty fun. Everyone, including Alex, cheered as her fighter punched Blake's fighter and knocked him over the edge of a balcony and onto the ground below. Her character jumped over the balcony and finished him off.

Blake raised an eyebrow. "You're certain you've never played this game before?"

"I'm a fast learner." Actually, she really didn't know what she was doing, she was just pushing the buttons as fast as she could.

They were about to play again when Alex stepped in. "I'm going to steal the ladies for a second, Blake. I want to show them around a little."

Blake nodded, then turned to Brooke. "Make certain you come back. I want a rematch."

Alex led them into the kitchen. It was the largest, fanciest kitchen Brooke had ever seen. It had an island in the middle that was covered with chips, salsa, soda and just about every other party food you could imagine.

"Help yourself to whatever you'd like. But go easy on the Cheesy Puffs. They're really spicy. They finished JJ off at the last party. Took him two hours to recover."

He led them outside, showed them the pool, hot tub, and cabana, then led them upstairs to show them the rest of the house. Every room was huge and completely immaculate. Even his bedroom. It was decorated with sports posters on the walls, including a large poster of Randy Johnson that was over his desk.

"You like Randy Johnson?" Brooke asked.

He nodded. "He's my hero. When I was little, I wanted to be just like him."

There was another room just down the hall from Alex's room. Alex tried to walk by and skip it, but the girls spotted it and headed inside.

Brooke was amazed. The entire room was filled with display cases, and every display case was filled with trophies. Alex's trophies. There were trophies in every shape, size, and color imaginable.

"How embarrassing," he said. "This room was my dad's idea. He's into this type of stuff."

"It's amazing," Brooke said.

"You can say that again," Naomi said.

Alex turned to Brooke, then pointed at a small podium in the exact middle of the room.

"You'll recognize that one."

Sitting on the podium was a dirt-stained baseball on a fancy display base. Brooke's eyes got big as she realized what it was. It was the ball she had caught to save Alex's no-hitter.

"Every time my dad has guests over," Alex said, "he brings them up here to show them that ball. It's his pride and joy. Mine, too."

They looked around a little more, then headed downstairs to rejoin the party. A couple more people had arrived, so Alex went to greet them and left the girls in the dining room to mingle with others. It was great fun. Brooke saw several people from her classes, and she met several new people, including some of the school's volleyball players. Apparently, they were Alyssa's friends and teammates.

Remarkably, however, she didn't see Alyssa, and that seemed strange. It was Alex's party, but his girlfriend wasn't there?

She mingled from room to room for several hours and even had her rematch with Blake. Remarkably, she won again. In the meantime, Naomi, Faith, and Aubrey spent the majority of the night hanging out with Blake, Terrell, JJ, and Skinny, and they all seemed to get along really well.

"You guys should come to one of our games," Naomi said. "I guarantee we'll put on a good show for you. So far we're in first place and we've only lost two games all year."

"Sweet," JJ said. "Sounds like a good time."

"I'm kind of worried," Terrell said. "If all of you girls play as well as Brooke, we guys are in big trouble. Before we know it, you'll take over the baseball team and we won't have anywhere to play."

"I don't think you have anything to worry about," Naomi said. "Brooke's the only one of us who's brave enough to try baseball."

"When you say brave," Faith asked, "do you mean crazy?"

"Completely."

They all laughed.

The highlight of the night came an hour later, when Alex asked Brooke to step out on the patio with him. She didn't really know what he wanted, but she really didn't care. If Alex asked her to do something, she did it. They walked over to the edge of the pool and stood there next to the water.

"I just wanted to thank you again for coming. It means a lot to me to have you here. I know this has been a tough season for you, dealing with the team and all, especially Blake."

"He seems okay with me now," she said, trying to put a light spin on things.

"You can say that again. You should have seen him that night Christian hit you in the head with that pitch. He was a wreck. He came over here for a while, but he wanted to go back out and hunt Christian down and kill him on the spot. It took all of us to calm him down and keep him from doing something stupid. As a result, I'm still worried about next week's game."

Brooke's eyes widened. At first she didn't know what he was talking about, but then she remembered. The next week was the big rematch with Alderwood. Their second game of the season against them.

"It's going to be ugly," Alex continued. "I know it. We've had issues with Christian in the past. All the way back to our Little League days. Twice we've had fights."

Brooke tipped her head to the side. "Fights? During games?"

Alex nodded. "It happens sometimes, especially when Christian is involved. One year he beaned JJ in the back. JJ got so mad he charged the mound. It was ugly. And another year he hit Skinny. I had to get ten stitches in my forehead after that fight. Right above my eye. I still have the scar if you look closely."

She did, and he was right. It was barely visible, but it was there, an inch or so above his right eye. She was amazed. It was probably the only flaw he had.

But then her thoughts returned to what he had just said. She still couldn't believe it. "Boys fight during games? Worse than what happened in the game where I got hit?"

"Sometimes. Don't you girls?"

Brooke shook her head. To be honest, she had never even heard of such a thing. Girls were notorious for being catty and talking bad about one another, including their own teammates, but she had never heard of a fight during a game before.

"What do you do?"

"What do you mean?"

"During a fight. What do you do?"

"Just punch anyone who comes near you. And I usually stay close to Blake or Skinny. That way, if I get in trouble, they can come to my rescue. And JJ is pretty good in a fight, too."

She nodded, but now she was really nervous about the upcoming game. When Coach West had originally asked her, and she had agreed to play for the baseball team, she hadn't known there would be any fights involved.

Alex clearly saw the concern in her eyes. "Enough of that. We'll worry about that next week, at the game. We're supposed to be having fun right now. So tell me a little about you. You're my star shortstop and I hardly know anything about you."

They made their way over to a couple of patio chairs and spent the next hour or so talking. She told him about her, and he told her about him. He was originally from

Laguna Beach but his family had moved to Seattle when he was ten. He had an older brother named James who was a sophomore at UCLA.

Brooke's heart stopped. Alex was so gorgeous she could hardly imagine what an older brother would look like.

Like all teenage boys, Alex loved loud, obnoxious music, action movies, and cars. He took her down to the garage so he could show her his car.

It was a silver Porsche. She didn't know exactly what model, but she really didn't care. To her, all Porsches were good Porsches.

"You want to go for a spin?"

Her answer was a little too enthusiastic, but she couldn't help herself. "Yeah."

It was the nicest car she had ever been in. All leather interior, rocking stereo, voice-activated ignition, the works. And it handled like a dream. They zipped around town taking corners with ease.

"Can you drive a clutch?"

She nodded.

"Give it a try." He stopped at a street light, hopped out, and switched seats with her.

She could hardly believe what was happening. She was about to drive a Porsche. It was a small step up, to say the least, from her Volkswagen Jetta.

But then something unexpected happened. She feathered the clutch wrong, the car lurched forward violently, and died. They laughed as Alex's phone, which he had set on the console between them, flew into the air and ended up on the floor at his feet.

"I forgot to mention the clutch is a little finicky. Until you get used to it, it's actually easier to take off in second."

She tried to follow his instructions and shift the car into second, but the gearshift wouldn't budge.

"The transmission is also a little finicky. Here, I'll show you."

He put his hand on top of hers and helped her shift the car into second. The minute his hand touched hers, her heart raced and the temperature in the car increased by at least ten degrees, probably more. She didn't fully recover until he removed his hand from hers.

"That should do it," he said. "Now give it a try."

And she did. The takeoff was a little rough, but it was fun nonetheless, and she actually managed to get the car moving. It had amazing power and cornered like a dream. She drove it around the block (twice), then headed back toward Alex's house. Aubrey greeted them the minute they pulled into the driveway.

"Tell me I did not see that."

"See what?" Brooke asked.

"You driving a Porsche. With Alex in the passenger seat next to you."

Brooke grinned. "You saw it."

"Oh my God. You're the coolest girl in the world."

Brooke and Alex returned to the patio and continued talking for another hour, maybe two. Unfortunately, things soured a little as the night wound on. It had been a great night, there was no denying that, but there was one thing Brooke had been curious about and had to ask.

"Where's Alyssa? I haven't seen her all night."

Alex's eyes got big for a second, then returned to normal. "She couldn't make it. Apparently something came up."

And then Brooke thought of something else. There was another person she hadn't seen all night.

"And what about Jamie? I've seen the rest of the guys tonight, but not him. It's weird to be here with the team but not have him around."

This time, Alex's eyes narrowed, and the tone of his voice changed dramatically. "Apparently, he couldn't make it, either. I'm going to get something to drink. Do you want something?"

"I'm okay."

Without another word, he walked away, into the house, and she didn't see him again that night.

Chapter 22

The baseball team had congregated in front of their dugout and Coach West was about to begin his traditional pre-practice speech, with instructions and plans for the day, when Blake stepped forward with a request.

"Some of the guys and I were talking, and we were wondering, we know it's unusual to take a day off from practice especially with a big game like Alderwood coming up this week, but the softball team has a game today and they invited us, and it means a lot to them because they finally got their new scoreboard—"

"They got their new scoreboard?" Coach West asked.

"Well, they've had it for a little while, but it just got installed last weekend, so today is the first day they're going to get to officially use it for a game, and it's a big deal to them, and well we'll make up today's practice tomorrow if you want with a double practice if you want, but it seems appropriate since Brooke came from the softball team and the other—"

He was probably going to ramble on forever so Alex came to his rescue. "What Blake is trying to say is we want to go to their game."

Coach West raised an eyebrow. "You guys have never shown any interest in the softball team before. Why now?"

In unison, they all looked at Brooke.

Coach West saw their reactions and nodded. "Is it true? Do you all want to go?"

It was unanimous. They didn't even have to think about it, since they had all discussed it as a group a few minutes before Coach West had arrived.

"And we're serious," Alex said. "We'll make up the practice tomorrow if you want, however you want. But this is a really big deal for the girls since they've waited a long time for that scoreboard. So it would be really nice to get to celebrate with them."

Coach West turned back to Blake. "This is a pretty unexpected request, especially coming from Blake, but at the same time it's a pretty good one as far as I'm concerned. And if I remember right, the girls are four-time defending WesCo South champions, right Brooke?"

Brooke corrected him instantly. "Five-time defending champions." She put extra emphasis on the word 'five.'

"Even better. Then they definitely deserve the attention. Blake's request is granted. Have fun, guys, and I'll see you tomorrow."

Brooke could hardly believe it. These were the same boys who originally wanted nothing to do with her. But now, they were skipping their own practice, two days before the big rematch with Alderwood, to support the softball team.

Coach West stopped her as she was rounding up her stuff. "I don't want to sound facetious, but I told you. I knew if you gave them a chance they'd come around. They're a good bunch. One of the best I've ever had."

Brooke's only response was a smile.

The girls on the softball team took a break from their warm-ups as the baseball team, with Blake at its front, walked up. Brooke watched, wide-eyed, as Faith stepped forward to greet them.

"You made it. We were all hoping you'd come."

"I told you Coach West would let us," Blake said. "He's really cool that way, and he had no problem with it at all. Oh, and I brought you this. You said you liked white roses."

In his left hand, he had a single, white, long-stemmed rose. Faith's eyes got big as he handed it to her.

"I got it during my lunch break," he continued, "and it's been sitting in my car ever since, so hopefully it didn't wilt too much."

"It's perfect, Blake. Thank you."

She was about to say something more but was interrupted when Coach Jennings called out from the field. The game was about to begin. The girls all turned and headed to their dugout. Brooke beat them there. She had to know what was going on with Faith and Blake.

"You and Blake? I can't believe it."

"He's so sweet," Faith said. "He called me the night after the party. I usually prefer texting, but Blake doesn't spell too well, so we talked instead, until 2:00 in the morning. And we would have talked even longer but my mom heard me and made me hang up and go to bed. He's the sweetest guy I've ever met."

"Blake?"

"Oh, I know. He seems all rough and gruff on the outside, but once you get to know him, he's just a big teddy bear."

Brooke almost fell over. Blake? A teddy bear?

"And guess what?" Faith said. "He can bench press over three hundred pounds. That's more than you and me combined."

She was about to say something more when Naomi rushed up. The smile on her face was almost as big as the smile on Faith's face. "You guys won't believe it. Remember how I was talking with Terrell at the party? Guess what? He just asked me out. We're going out tonight, right after the game."

Brooke was in heaven. She had never seen her friends so happy. They were completely ecstatic.

She turned to Aubrey. "What about you?"

Aubrey's answer was instant. "I'm working on it." She turned to the bleachers, where all the boys were now sitting, waiting anxiously for the game to begin. As if on cue, JJ waved at her.

Coach Jennings called the girls over for their traditional pregame meeting. Brooke started to walk over to take her place with the boys when Jamie stood up in the bleachers and called out to Coach Jennings.

"Coach. Is Brooke still on your roster?"

Coach Jennings looked a little puzzled at first, but then nodded. "Actually, I think she is. I meant to remove her when she agreed to play for you guys, but to be honest I forgot completely about it."

"Then she's still eligible to play for you if she's available, right?"

Coach Jennings nodded. "Technically, she is."

"She's one of us now, a baseball player, but we're a generous group so we'd be willing to loan her to you for a day if you'd like."

Skinny stood up next to Jamie. "And I'll vouch for her. She won't let you down."

They all laughed.

Coach Jennings smiled and turned to Brooke. "What do you think? We could always use an All-Star shortstop."

Brooke was tempted but hesitant. "The game's about to begin, and I left all my gear in my car. I dropped it off on the way over here."

"Leave that to me," Terrell said. He grabbed Brooke's keys from her, darted across the field to the parking lot, grabbed her bag out of her trunk, and was back in a flash.

Brooke laughed. "I guess now I've got no choice."

Everyone cheered.

It was the fastest uniform change Brooke had ever made, and she was still struggling to get her left cleat on as she took the field to start the game. And then she noticed it for the first time.

The new scoreboard. It was in left field, in the exact same position as the old scoreboard, but it was at least twice as big, and it was one of the fanciest scoreboards she had ever seen. It had a video screen on one side where each player's name, number, and stats appeared, and another screen below it where a photo of each player appeared as she came up to bat.

Naomi saw her admiring it. "What do you think?"

Brooke's answer was instant. "I love it."

The game began and it was unrivaled fun. With all the boys there, it was the largest crowd the softball team had ever had. And it was a rowdy crowd. The boys cheered with every pitch, and they went absolutely bonkers when Brooke made a running catch in foul territory to end the third inning. Overall, she had a solid game, including a single and a sacrifice fly to score a run, but to be perfectly honest the night belonged to the other girls. It was their first time playing in front of the boys and they were absolutely determined to impress them, and boy did they. Aubrey went 3-3 with three singles, Naomi went 2-4 with a double and a triple, and Faith went 3-4 with two singles and a massive home run that went right over the new scoreboard in left. It was the longest shot Brooke had ever seen her hit.

Blake was all smiles as he watched Faith's home run fly into the distance. "That's my type of girl."

It was a complete blowout. Silver Lake won 10-0.

Chapter 23

It was the big day. The rematch with Alderwood. Brooke was nervous, and she was still worried about what Alex had told her the weekend before at his party. The info about the possible fight. She had thought about it a lot, to be honest way too much, but she still didn't know what she'd do if a fight actually happened.

Coach West called Blake over to him just before the game began. Brooke was at the opposite end of the dugout, watching Alderwood's players warm up in the infield, but she could still hear his words as though he were standing right next to her. "I'm going to change the batting order today, Blake. Unlike normal, you're going to take the spot after Brooke."

"After Brooke?" Blake asked. That was unusual. Since he was the biggest player on the team and their main power hitter, he usually batted in the fourth spot, right in front of their other power hitter, Skinny.

"I want you in the on-deck circle when Brooke bats. That way, if Christian throws at her again, you'll be closer to the mound and can get there quicker."

Blake smiled. "And?"

Coach West looked straight at him, right into his eyes. Clearly, he wanted to make certain he understood his intentions. "If he throws at her, I want you to take care of things the old-fashioned way. Understood?"

Blake's answer was immediate, and it was nothing more than a simple nod. Clearly, he knew what Coach West meant. Brooke was new to the baseball world, but even so she was pretty certain she knew what it meant, too.

"And Blake," Coach West continued, "since I'm your coach, if anyone found out I gave you instructions like that, there would be repercussions. And they would be bad."

Blake nodded. "You never told me nothing, Coach."

"You're a good boy, Blake. Do me a favor today. Take care of your teammate, whatever the cost."

"Will do."

Now Brooke was really nervous. She could hardly believe it. Alex wasn't the only one who thought something bad was going to happen. Coach West thought so, too, and he was so concerned about it he had gone out of his way to make preparations.

Luckily, however, the game went fine for the first two innings. Just like the first game between Alderwood and Silver Lake, it was a classic pitcher's duel between Christian and Alex. They were the best pitchers in the league, and they were both pitching like it. Neither boy had given up a single hit when Brooke stepped up to the plate in the bottom of the third inning.

Normally, Brooke loved batting. It was one of her favorite things in the whole world. Sometimes, in big games, it even gave her goosebumps. But not on that day. On that day, she was scared breathless, literally. She wasn't even breathing. The minute she stepped into the batter's box, she started having flashbacks of her first at-bat against Christian. She could still hear the sickly sound of the ball as it struck the side of her helmet. A loud, hollow crack, followed by a dull thud as she hit the ground, followed by a clank as her bat landed next to her. Her forehead started to throb just thinking about it.

And Christian didn't make her feel any better. He stood on the mound, staring down at her from above, smiling menacingly. He looked like some type of wild animal that was closing in on its helpless prey.

Blake stood to the side, in the on-deck circle, watching everything unfold. He saw how Blake was looking at Brooke and decided to give him a warning.

"Don't even think about it, Christian."

Brooke had never heard him sound so menacing. It was even scarier than the way he had talked to her at the beginning of the season.

Christian smiled at Blake, then turned his attention back to Brooke. "How sweet. They got you a bodyguard."

Brooke had no interest in responding, none at all, and instead raised her bat, preparing herself for his first pitch, which was an absolute fireball. She swung at it and missed badly.

She wasn't happy she had missed the pitch, but she was relieved nonetheless. It had been absolutely beastly, but it had been straight down the middle of the plate, and not aimed anywhere near her head.

She snuck a quick peek at her dad, who was sitting in his normal spot in the stands. He looked every bit as nervous as she felt. His face was as white as a ghost. Clearly, he was worried about what was going to happen, too.

The second pitch was low and away, so Brooke laid off of it for ball one. The third pitch was low as well, but this time a little closer to the plate. The fourth, however, was a replay of the first, lightning fast and straight down the middle. Unlike the first pitch, however, Brooke was ready and she turned and hit it as hard as she could, straight back at the mound, straight back at Christian. He lunged at it but missed it by an inch. It shot into center field for a single.

Brooke was ecstatic, since she had somehow managed to get a hit off him, which was Silver Lake's first of the day, but he wasn't happy, not at all. He was disappointed in himself and downright upset he had given up a hit to a girl. He paced around the mound and slapped his glove against his thigh.

Unfortunately, Blake struck out to end the inning, and the pitcher's duel continued from there. The game was still scoreless when Brooke got her next at-bat in the bottom of the sixth inning.

This time, she was a little more comfortable stepping up to the plate. Christian hadn't tried to hit her the first time, and he hadn't thrown a single pitch anywhere near her. As such, maybe he wouldn't try that time, either. Maybe all of her concerns had been for nothing, and maybe nothing ugly would transpire after all. Maybe it would just be a good, old-fashioned, well-played game.

She could never be so lucky. The very first pitch came right at her, but unlike in the first game, it didn't hit her square in the head. She somehow managed to turn, just a little, and the pitch only grazed the side of her helmet. Even so, it was enough to knock her to the ground, not so much a result of the force of the blow but more a result of her being off balance when it made contact. Luckily, however, she wasn't hurt badly, not really at all, so she only stayed on the ground for a few seconds. But when she got back up and looked around, she could hardly believe what she saw. The entire infield was chaos. The minute she had gone down, Blake had thrown his bat to the side, darted from his spot in the on-deck circle, and charged the mound like a gladiator rushing into battle. Currently, he was on top of Christian and was pounding him with both hands like an enraged ape. In the meantime, Alderwood's catcher and first baseman were on top of him, punching him, and Skinny, Terrell, and JJ were on top of them. A few feet to the side was another pile of bodies, including mostly everyone else on both teams. Jamie had Alderwood's center fielder pinned to the ground, and Alex was in a nasty shoving match with their shortstop and second baseman. The umpires and coaches were trying desperately to break it up and pull the players apart but they were outnumbered and weren't making much progress.

Brooke didn't know what to do. She was just standing there, by herself at home plate, in complete shock, since she had narrowly avoided another trip to the emergency room. She felt absolutely horrible, just standing there by herself, doing nothing, while the boys were fighting to protect her. Not knowing what else to do, she dropped her bat and wandered slowly toward the nearest pile of boys, the one with Blake, Christian, Skinny, and countless others. She didn't know what she was going to do when she got there, but she felt she needed to go anyway, if nothing else just to show some support by being there.

When she got there, however, something unexpected happened. Christian loomed up in front of her. Two of Alderwood's players had somehow managed to pull Blake back, temporarily, and as a result Christian had wrested himself free. Blake had clearly gotten in some good shots beforehand. Blood ran from the corner of Christian's mouth and one eye was swollen shut. Regardless, he was laughing hysterically, maniacally, as though he was somehow enjoying the whole sordid thing. Brooke was absolutely terrified when she saw his appearance, and absolutely dumbfounded when she saw how he was acting, and the combination of everything snapped something inside of her. Without a single thought, she did the one thing she thought she'd never do. She waited until he turned to face her, then punched him in the face as hard as she could. Her blow landed perfectly, right at the top of his nose between his eyes, and there was a loud crack. He fell backward and was unconscious the second he hit the ground.

Chapter 24

Brooke was a legend at Silver Lake High School. Word of what she had done spread through the school like wildfire. She was the girl who had knocked out the infamous Christian Parkinson, the most hated rival the school's baseball team had ever had. And she had done it with a single punch.

Unfortunately, she wasn't allowed to be there to enjoy her newfound fame. The morning after the big fight, the school's athletic director suspended every member of the team for their roles in the fracas, and they got differing lengths of time based on each player's particular role. Blake got the longest suspension, a week, Brooke got the next longest, three days, and everyone else, including Coach West, got a day. But it didn't really matter that much to Brooke, since she needed some time away from school to recover emotionally and process what had happened. She still couldn't believe what she had done, and she actually felt pretty bad about it, since she wasn't the type of person who liked fighting and she had never intended to punch anyone, even a creep like Christian. At the same time, however, she didn't get too down on herself and everyone else seemed to think that what she had done was awesome. By noon of the first day of her suspension, she had received 354 texts from 152 different people, all wanting to know the specific details of the fight.

"What happened?"

"Did you get hurt?"

"How did you feel when the pitch hit you?"

"Was it as bad as the first time?"

"How long did it take you to get back up?"

"How long did it take you to get to the mound after you got hit?"

"How did you feel when you punched Christian?"

"How long was he on the ground?"

"How long was he unconscious?"

"Did you punch anyone else?"

"There's a kid at school who has been bullying me. Will you punch him for me?"

That last message was her favorite.

Like all teenage girls, Brooke loved texting, but she actually started to get a little frustrated because her phone was literally on the verge of exploding all day long. The messages would not stop, and in the time it took her to respond to one, she'd get five more.

Her Facebook account was no different. In one day, she got new friend requests from 120 different people, and most of them were people she had never met or heard of before. Some of them were even kids from schools other than Silver Lake, other local high and middle schools, but they had heard what had happened and wanted to be friends with her anyway.

If the texts, e-mails, Facebook posts, and Twitter tweets weren't enough, she also got a nickname. Everyone started calling her "Boxin' Brooke" and the members of the school's wrestling team actually voted to add her to the team as an honorary member. Aubrey was a big fan of that particular accolade.

"Does that mean you can show up at wrestling practice and roll around with the boys on the floor?"

Brooke shook her head. "I don't think that's what it means, Faith. Nor would I do it even if I could."

As far as Brooke was concerned, the most surprising thing that happened was what occurred at home. She couldn't believe it, since her dad was usually so uptight and strict with her, but even he was impressed. At first, he tried to do the proper grown-up thing and tell her that fighting was unacceptable and was never a good solution to a problem, but he couldn't keep up the charade for long.

"I couldn't believe it, Brooke. Where'd you learn to punch like that?"

She shrugged. She hadn't learned it anywhere. She'd just done it.

"That kid never had a chance," her dad continued. "I bet you broke his nose. It was awesome."

Later that day, she heard him in his den, speaking with one of his friends on his phone. He had his laptop on the desk in front of him. "Go to YouTube. What? Yeah, some kid took a video of it using his phone. The quality's pretty bad and it's pretty dark, but you can still see things anyway. Search for baseball babe punches pitcher. Did you find it? Good, now watch carefully. Right at the end you'll see Brooke. See her, there she is, walking toward the mound. Wait. Wait. Down he goes! Can you believe it? What?" He paused for a second. "Oh, I know. It's incredible. Look at her form when she punches that kid. She reminds me of Tyson back in his prime."

Brooke couldn't help but laugh. In a strange sort of way, and despite the fact she didn't really like the nickname, it was kinda fun being Boxin' Brooke. The only bad thing, however, was her right hand. She had punched Christian so hard she had broken two of her nails, the ones on her middle and index fingers, and chipped two more.

That sucked. Especially since she had just gotten her nails done a couple of days before.

Chapter 25

Brooke sat in the school cafeteria, eating lunch with Naomi, Aubrey, and Faith. It was her first day back following her suspension. Faith was in the middle of complaining about her French teacher, since apparently he had misplaced one of her assignments for the third time that year, when Jamie walked by. He didn't say anything but his appearance immediately got their attention. Faith stopped her story mid-sentence. Everyone remained silent until he was out of earshot.

"I still can't believe it," Naomi said.

"Me, neither," Faith said. "It totally blows my mind."

Brooke looked at them. She had no idea what they were talking about.

"You haven't heard?" Aubrey asked. "Where've you been? It's been all over school the past few days. It's almost as big as you punching Christian."

"I've been at home," Brooke said. "I was suspended, remember?"

"Oh yeah. Anyway, do you remember awhile back when I told you Alex got mad at Alyssa because she went to a movie with another guy? Guess what? That guy was Jamie."

Brooke's mouth fell open. Now it all made sense. She couldn't believe she hadn't figured it out earlier. The game against Edmonds when Alex had barked at Jamie for making an error. Now she knew why Alex had acted so out of character and had been so mad. It had nothing to do with the error. It was about Alyssa. He was mad because she had gone out with Jamie. And the night at Alex's party. No wonder Jamie and Alyssa weren't there and Alex hadn't wanted to talk about it. They were probably together.

As if on cue, Aubrey added, "Apparently they went out again."

"No way," Faith and Naomi said.

Aubrey continued. "Apparently Alyssa told the girls on the volleyball team she really likes Jamie and she's thinking about breaking up with Alex so she can be with him. She even went to Alex's house one night to do it, but Alex got so upset she chickened out and didn't go through with it. And now she's really confused and doesn't know what to do."

She wasn't the only one. Brooke just sat there, absolutely speechless, her head spinning. She couldn't help but wonder how this was going to affect the baseball team.

Since both Alex and Jamie were on the team, would there be repercussions?

She got her answer quickly. That night, right after practice, things got ugly. She was loading her bag into the trunk of her car when she heard a sound nearby and looked up. Most of the baseball team had already left, so the parking lot was empty with the exception of two cars, a Porsche and a Camaro, parked side-by-side under a large tree. Alex and Jamie stood between the cars, talking about something, and they didn't look too happy. Both boys' faces were red. Brooke knew she shouldn't eavesdrop on their conversation, but after what she had learned at school earlier in the day, she couldn't help herself. And immediately upon hearing their words she got worried, because the conversation wasn't pleasant. Not at all.

"You need to stay away from her," Alex said. His eyes were really intense and he was clearly frustrated. "I'm not going to tell you again, Jamie."

"She's not your property," Jamie responded. "She can do whatever she wants. And see whomever she wants. If she wants to see me, then she can."

"You and I have been friends a long time. I've never asked you for much. But I'm asking you now for one thing – stay away from her. You know she's my girlfriend."

"Have you spoken to her lately? Today?"

"I don't need to. I need to speak with you. And you need to do what I say. You need to stay away from her. I'm not going to tell you again."

"Or what?"

Brooke's heart was about to break. She was watching the two nicest boys on the team, the two boys she cared the most about, fighting with one another. And it was getting really intense really fast. The tone of their voices made it clear things were going to explode.

And it did. Alex pushed Jamie with both hands, right in the chest, as hard as he could. Jamie fell back against his Camaro but was able to catch himself before falling completely to the ground. He righted himself, then turned back to face Alex. There was rage in his eyes.

The fight was on. Alex got in a couple of quick blows, including one that hit Jamie in the mouth and bloodied his lip pretty badly. But Jamie turned the tide quickly. He wasn't as tall as Alex, but he was a lot bulkier and a lot more muscular. He punched Alex in the stomach, then in the chest, then in the stomach again. Alex fell to the ground gasping for breath. Jamie jumped on top of him and started to pummel him repeatedly.

Brooke panicked and darted toward them as fast as she could. She had to do something. She couldn't let this continue and she got there just in time. Jamie was about to punch Alex right in the face when she grabbed his arm from behind.

"Jamie, please stop."

Luckily, that was all it took. The sound of her voice snapped Jamie out of his frenzy and he instantly returned to normal. He covered his eyes in shame as he looked down at Alex and realized what he had done.

"Alex. I'm sorry. I never thought this would happen."

He got up, climbed into his Camaro, and drove off. A tear ran down his cheek as he disappeared from view.

Brooke turned to Alex and tried to help him up but he pushed her away. He was furious. He climbed up and got into his Porsche.

"Alex. Are you okay?"

He spit blood from his mouth. "I'm fine."

"Where are you going?"

"To find Alyssa. I'm going to put an end to this one way or another."

He raced off.

Chapter 26

Brooke paced from one side of her bedroom to the other for most of the evening. She called Aubrey and Naomi, and told them what had happened between Alex and Jamie, but they didn't know what to do either. But then she got a call from a number she didn't recognize. Usually, she didn't answer unfamiliar numbers, but this time she did, hoping it was someone who knew something, anything, about Alex or Jamie. And luckily it was. It was Blake.

"Brooke, I got your number from Faith. I hope you don't mind me calling, but anyway we guys are at Alex's house right now and we need you to come over as fast as you can. Alex locked himself in his room and he won't come out. He says he's quitting the team."

"What happened?"

"He went over to Alyssa's to confront her about Jamie and she broke up with him. He's a mess now and he won't listen to anyone. We're hoping he'll listen to you."

She didn't know why he would, why he would treat her any differently than any other member of the team, but at the same time she had to do something. Sitting in her room, doing nothing, was driving her crazy. As such, she jumped in her car and drove to his house as fast as she could. She was amazed she didn't get a speeding ticket on the way. When she got there, several members of the team, including JJ, Terrell, Skinny, and Blake were in the upstairs hall outside Alex's room. They looked terrible, like they were worried sick.

"He won't even respond anymore," Blake said. "I don't know what to do. JJ and Terrell are worried he's going to hurt himself. They want me to kick the door in."

Brooke thought for a minute. "Where are his parents? Can they help us?"

Blake shook his head. "They're in Palm Springs for the week."

Wonderful, Brooke thought. *So much for that.*

Blake looked at her closely. "Do you think I should kick the door in? Like JJ wants?"

To be perfectly honest, Brooke didn't know what to do. She had never been in that type of situation before. But kicking in the door seemed pretty severe, so she wanted to try something else before they went to that extreme.

"Let me try something first." She walked up to Alex's door and confirmed it was locked, which was actually a pretty stupid thing to do, since they already knew it was.

"Alex," she said through the door. "It's me, Brooke. Are you okay?"

She listened for a minute, hoping for a response, but there was none.

"Alex. Please let me in."

Again, there was nothing but silence.

She was really starting to sweat now. She was nervous, and all the boys were watching her intently, hoping she could do something, anything, and that was making her even more nervous. Blake stood at the far end of the hall, and much to Brooke's shock and dismay he had started to hit his forehead against the nearby wall.

She was about to give up and tell Blake to go through with it and kick in the door when she thought of something. It was probably a long shot, and she doubted it would work, but she had no other alternatives. She turned back to the door.

"Alex, do you remember that time, awhile back, when we were sitting in the dugout and you thanked me for saving your no-hitter? You told me if I ever needed anything, anything at all, I just needed to ask and you would make it happen. Well I'm asking now. I need you to open the door and let me in."

There was a painfully long silence. At first she thought it hadn't worked, her plan had failed and her plea had fallen on deaf ears, but amazingly it did. The lock clicked, and the door opened just a hair, just enough for her to squeeze in. She heard Alex's voice from behind it.

"Brooke can come in. But only Brooke."

She didn't know what else to do, so she took one last look at Blake and the other boys, then stepped through the door and closed it softly behind her. She felt no need to lock it so she left it unlocked. By the time she got fully inside Alex was back on his bed, lying on his back, staring blankly at the ceiling. His eyes were bloodshot and he'd clearly been crying. A lamp was on the floor next to the bed and it was in pieces. Its shade was near the far wall and several chunks of its base were littered over the carpet.

She didn't know what to say, so she just sat down on the bed next to him.

"You shouldn't have come," he said. "This isn't your concern."

"Yes it is. I may be the new kid on the team, but it's still my team. And if a member of the team is in trouble, I'm in trouble."

He didn't know what to say in response, so he said nothing. Instead, he rolled onto his stomach and buried his face in a pillow.

"The guys are worried about you," Brooke said. "Just about everyone is out there. Blake is so upset he's banging his head against the wall. I've never seen anything like it."

"He does that sometimes."

"He told me you're quitting the team."

"I have no choice. I can't go on like this after all that's happened. I'm a wreck. I can't focus at all. There's no way I can pitch. You guys will be better off without me."

"No we won't. We need you, Alex. And not just for your pitching. You're our leader. Everyone looks up to you and respects you. And we care about you. If we didn't, why would we all be here right now? From what I've heard, things are getting pretty hot between Blake and Faith. I bet he'd rather be with her tonight, at a movie or dinner or something, but he's not. He's here with you, and he's worried out of his mind."

There was a long silence, but then Alex rolled over, once again revealing his face. Brooke hoped that was a good sign, a sign she was making some progress with him.

He sighed. "Blake. He's always been the sensitive one. Every group has one. One time, back in Little League, JJ broke his leg and Blake was so worried he started crying."

Brooke's mouth nearly fell open. "Blake cried?"

Alex nodded. "It's happened a few times over the years. I remember another time in Summer League. Skinny got hurt and had to be taken away in an ambulance. They couldn't settle Blake down until they told him he could ride along in the ambulance with Skinny to make certain he would be okay."

Brooke was dumbfounded. "I never pictured Blake crying."

"Don't tell him I told you. Or he'll beat me up for sure. He's got a rep to maintain, you know. He's supposed to be the tough guy."

"You've got nothing to worry about. I won't say a thing."

There was a long, awkward silence. They basically just sat there looking at one another.

"How are you feeling?" It was a stupid thing to ask but it was the only thing she could think of.

He gave her a funny look, as if to say, "What do you think?"

"Sorry. That was a dumb question. Blake said things didn't go well with Alyssa."

"She broke up with me. She started crying. She said she was sorry, she didn't mean to hurt me, but she just couldn't help it. She's got feelings for Jamie now."

Brooke nodded. She didn't know what to say. Luckily, however, Alex continued.

"I don't blame her. Jamie's a great guy. We've been friends forever, way back to the first grade. I can't believe we got into a fight. I'm sorry you had to see that."

"It's no big deal. I'm just glad neither of you got hurt." Then she remembered the blood coming from Alex's mouth when she last saw him. "Did you?"

"I'll live. I guess I should have seen this coming a long time ago. Alyssa and I have had some issues for a while now. At least six months, maybe more. I noticed something was different between us even before she started seeing Jamie. It was like the spark had gone out between us. But I wasn't willing to give up. She and I had gone out for so long, almost two years, and I thought things would eventually get better if I just stayed patient. And one day I thought we would get—"

His words trailed off. He didn't want to finish the sentence.

"I guess I was just being silly," he continued. "What do our parents say? Acting like a teenager?"

Brooke groaned. Her dad had used that expression several times over the years, and she had never liked it. Just thinking about it made her angry.

There was another long silence. Finally, Alex spoke again.

"I guess all things end eventually. Including relationships. Have you ever been through something like this?"

Brooke shook her head. She didn't like to admit it, but her longest relationship had only lasted six months, and it hadn't really been that serious.

"Not really. But I can still understand."

"I still remember when I first started seeing Alyssa. Back when we were sophomores. There was word around school Farrah Hemingway wanted to hook up with me. Do you know her?"

Brooke shook her head. She had never heard of Farrah Hemingway before.

"She was a senior at the time. She was the captain of the cheerleading team. She had just broken up with her boyfriend and was looking for a replacement. The guys said I would be a legend if I hooked up with her, since she was an older girl and all. And I'll give her credit. She was hot. She was tall and thin, with long legs and huge—"

"I don't need all the details," Brooke interrupted. She put special emphasis on the word 'all.'

"Sorry. Anyway, the guys wanted me to hook up with her, but then I met Alyssa and she was so perfect. We got along so well, and her smile was amazing. All she had to do was look at me and my whole brain would go fuzzy. I know it probably sounds stupid but it's true."

Brooke was speechless. To her, it didn't sound stupid at all. Actually, it was one of the most touching things she had ever heard.

Much to her surprise, Alex sat up, and he looked a little better. Not much, but a little. Maybe talking was helping him.

"I bet you never thought it would come to this."

"What?"

"When you joined the team. I bet you never thought you'd end up sitting in the pitcher's bedroom trying to convince him to stay on the team."

Brooke smiled. "A lot of things have happened this year I didn't expect. I never expected to have such a tough time finding my place on the team. And I never expected to get hit in the head by a pitch. And I definitely never expected to punch out an opposing pitcher. I still can't believe I did that. But anyway, I guess that's the way it goes sometimes. Sometimes you just have to deal with what happens and move on the best you can. Life isn't perfect. It doesn't always go according to plan."

"I'm not as strong as you. A girl who plays baseball? It doesn't get any stronger than that. You must be made of steel, Brooke. Nothing can break you. But I'm not like you. I'm not certain I can move on."

"You can. And you're stronger than you realize, Alex. You just need to give it some time and give yourself some credit. Everything will be okay. I hope."

"I hope?"

"It's not like I have a crystal ball or something. But I have faith. And you need to have faith, too."

He sighed, then nodded.

"Can we head back out now?" Brooke asked. "With the other guys? They're probably wondering how things are going in here. And I think I can still hear Blake hitting his head on the wall."

They listened, and sure enough she was right. There was a steady thumping coming from down the hall.

"I hope he doesn't need stitches again," Alex said.

"Stitches?"

"It happened once. A few years back. He got really upset when he struck out to end a game. We spent two hours in the ER."

He stood up, straightened out his clothes to make them as presentable as possible, and together they walked into the hall.

Chapter 27

The next day, Brooke's softball team, the Angels, had a tournament in Tacoma, a city about half an hour south of Seattle. Their first game was against a team from southern Oregon called the Pony Express. It was a good game, and the Angels trailed most of the way, but they came back to win 3-2 in the final inning. Brooke got a single and Faith hit a home run.

Brooke looked over at Faith as they headed to another field for their second game of the day. "Where's all this power coming from lately?"

"Blake's been giving me some tips. He knows a lot about power hitting."

Brooke smiled. She should have known better.

Aubrey, who was walking to their side, joined the conversation. "How's Alex today? Have you spoken to him?"

Brooke nodded. "He called me first thing this morning. He's doing okay. He still seems a little sad, which I guess is to be expected, but he's definitely better than yesterday."

"That's good. Hopefully he'll be back to normal soon. We can't have the hottest boy at school moping around all the time."

They all chuckled. Leave it to Aubrey to make light of things and make such a silly remark. They continued along for another minute or so before Aubrey spoke again.

"I still can't believe it. Alyssa had two of the hottest boys at school fighting over her. And it was an actual fist fight. It's so romantic. She's definitely the coolest girl in school."

Brooke stopped in her tracks. "Wait a minute. I thought you said I was the coolest girl in school? Since I drove Alex's Porsche and I punched Christian."

"That was last week. This week, Alyssa is the coolest girl."

Brooke sighed. She had no choice but to agree with the old expression, "Fame is a fleeting thing." Apparently, her fifteen minutes had already come and went.

"So anyway," Faith said. "What's your status?"

Brooke raised an eyebrow. She didn't know what Faith was talking about.

"With Alex? Now that he and Alyssa are history, the door is wide open for someone new to take her place. Someone like you."

Brooke's heart missed a beat. She had been so busy lately, so preoccupied with everything that had happened, she hadn't even had a chance to think about it. Could she really have a chance with Alex? To be his next girlfriend?

"I think he likes you," Aubrey said.

"Me, too," Faith said. "I saw how he was looking at you at the party. There was a definite sparkle in his eyes. But he was holding himself back because he was confused about his relationship with Alyssa. But now that that's over, who knows? Maybe he'll decide to give you a try."

Brooke was hopeful, since she really liked Alex, but she didn't get much time to think about it. Something, or to be more precise, someone, caught her eye.

The tournament they were competing in included teams of all ages from multiple leagues, and there was a Little League team playing a game on a nearby field. Brooke watched as the team's shortstop, a little girl with a long, black ponytail, fielded a grounder and whipped it effortlessly to first. Brooke recognized her instantly.

It was Kat. Jamie's sister.

She looked in the stands, and there he sat, watching her attentively.

"Way to go, sis," he said as she trotted off the field to end the inning. "Great throw."

As expected, Kat was all smiles as she soaked up the compliment.

Brooke was so jealous. If only she had had an older brother to give her compliments like that.

She turned to Faith and Aubrey. They were busy talking and hadn't noticed Jamie. "I'll catch up with you guys in a couple of minutes, okay?"

"Where are you going?" Faith asked.

"Over there. There's someone I want to talk to. I won't be long."

They shrugged and headed along. The second they were gone, Brooke turned and headed over to Jamie. He was watching Kat take her practice swings and didn't see her until she sat down in the bleachers right next to him. His eyes got big the minute he saw her.

"How are they doing?" she asked.

"Good. They're winning 4-3." He smiled at her, but he was clearly uncomfortable. She could tell it in his voice. "Kat has a single and two doubles."

"Sweet." She paused for a second before continuing. "And how about you? How are you?"

It took him a second to respond. "I'm okay. And I'm sorry about yesterday. Thank you for breaking up that fight. I don't know what I was thinking. I lost my mind for a couple of minutes."

"It's okay. Things happen. I'm just glad you and Alex are okay."

"Me, too." He paused for a second and turned to Kat as she walked up to the plate. "Hands up, kid. Stay aggressive up there."

He turned back to Brooke. "Alex called me about an hour ago. I was so surprised I didn't know what to do and I almost didn't answer. He apologized for everything. He said it was all his fault and he should have never acted the way he did."

He paused for a second as the pitcher whipped the ball to the plate. It was a nasty fastball. Kat swung and missed.

"That's okay," Jamie called out to her. "You'll get the next one." He turned back to Brooke. "I told Alex it was all my fault. I should have never gone out with Alyssa in the first place. I knew she was his girlfriend. But I just couldn't help it. There's something about her, something magical. Her eyes are incredible and her smile is to die for."

Brooke chuckled. Where had she heard that before?

They watched as Kat swung and missed again.

"Strike two," the umpire called.

"What did Alex say?" Brooke asked.

"He said he cared too much about Alyssa to do anything to hurt her, and he wants our relationship, his and mine, to go back to the way it was, back before this whole thing began, so he's going to do his best to move on. And he even wished us well. It really surprised me at first, but now that I've had some time to think about it, it shouldn't have. Alex is a good guy, and he always has been. He always puts everyone else's needs before his own."

Brooke had never felt so relieved. Nothing made her happier than hearing Alex and Jamie were mending their relationship and going to be friends again.

Jamie watched Kat for a few seconds, as she fouled away two consecutive pitches, then turned abruptly back to Brooke. "Can I ask you something? Did you have something to do with this? Did you talk to him?"

Brooke grinned. "We may have discussed a few things."

"Then I owe you. I can't thank you enough, Brooke. You're a savior."

Their eyes got big as Kat turned on the next pitch and hit it as hard as she could.

They cheered as the ball raced toward the outfield fence and cleared it by at least twenty feet. It was the longest home run Brooke had ever seen a ten-year-old hit.

"She's an amazing young lady," Brooke said.

"She's not the only one," Jamie said.

Chapter 28

The whole team was excited. There was nothing quite like the state playoffs. It was do-or-die time. If they won the day's game, they would advance to the next round and still have a chance at the state title. If they lost, however, their season would be over and they could start making plans for the offseason.

The game was in Mount Vernon, a city about sixty minutes north of Seattle. It was a long bus ride but it gave Coach West plenty of time to brief them and prepare them for the day's opponent.

"From what I hear, Mount Vernon is strong top-to-bottom, but their key player is their pitcher, a sophomore named Ned O'Bannon. He doesn't throw very hard, but he's got a lot of junk pitches. His curve is supposed to be absolutely wicked, so we're going to have to be really patient at the plate today, and really disciplined, and wait for him to make an error."

It didn't take them long to find out that Ned was exactly as advertised. During Brooke's first at-bat, she was completely fooled by his pitches. His first pitch was a nasty screwball, his second was an even nastier curveball, and the third was something she had never seen before. It was some type of change-curve-screw combination, if there was such a thing. As a result, she struck out quickly.

And she wasn't the only one who struggled. Blake was a mess. He was by far their best power hitter, and he led the team in home runs and runs batted in, but he had one major flaw. He couldn't hit curveballs to save his life. Like any good pitcher, Ned discovered his weakness and struck him out three times in a row.

After Blake's final at-bat, he was so frustrated he threw his helmet against the dugout's wall. Part of it broke off and bounced to the side.

Luckily, Brooke fared a little better as the game progressed. She struck out again during her second at-bat, but during her third she managed to get a piece of a breaking ball-curve-slider-changeup and she hit it into right field for a single.

And it was really good timing, because Jamie was up after her. And Jamie was their best batter by far. He didn't have as much power as Blake, but he had no 'holes' in his swing. He led the team in almost every offensive category: hits, walks, on-base percentage, batting average, and total bases.

No pitch fooled him for long, and he already had two hits in the game. Ned's pitches, as strange as they were, weren't a concern for him.

As such, he wasted no time. He hit the first pitch all the way to the outfield wall. Brooke took off from first the second he hit it, knowing she could easily make it to third, but then something unexpected happened. Mount Vernon's center fielder made a mistake and played the rebound off the wall wrong, and as a result he bobbled the ball momentarily. Coach West saw the bobble and immediately waved her on. She rounded third and headed for home as the center fielder scooped up the ball and made a desperate attempt to throw her out at the plate.

Brooke wasn't the fastest player on the team, not even close, but she was fast enough. She slid under the catcher's tag for the go-ahead run.

And that was all it took. Alex struck out Mount Vernon's final three batters and they won 1-0.

The following rounds of the playoffs were more of the same. All of the games were close, but Silver Lake always found a way to win in the end. Skinny was the hero of the second game, with two singles and the game-winning home run, Alex was the hero of the third, with fifteen strikeouts, Jamie was the hero of the fourth, with three singles including the game winner in the bottom of the seventh, and Terrell stole the show in the fifth, with a great diving catch in center field that saved at least two runs, probably more.

And before they knew it, they were in the championship game.

Chapter 29

The team was totally jacked. This was the day they had been waiting for all season long. The state's championship game. Every team in the state of Washington wanted to make it to this game, but only two teams had. Unfortunately, the other team was Alderwood. They, too, had played a lot of tough, close games, but they had always managed to prevail and had made their way through the playoffs. As such, Brooke and her teammates had no choice but to face their greatest nemesis one final time, with the greatest prize, the state's championship trophy, at stake. As they got off their bus, they saw Christian nearby, warming up. He wore a protective mask over his face.

"What's wrong with your nose?" Skinny asked. "You get punched by a girl?"

Everyone laughed.

But Brooke wasn't laughing for long. She was nervous. This was one of the biggest games she had ever played in, and like always she was worried about Christian. Was he going to throw at her again? If he was mad at her before, he was probably furious now.

Everyone was there to watch the game, including her dad and all of the girls from the softball team. It was one of the biggest crowds she had ever played in front of.

The umpires discussed things with both teams before the game began, and they were much stricter than normal.

"We're aware of the history between these teams," the head umpire said, "and we'll tolerate nothing today. Anyone gets out of line, in any way, they'll be ejected immediately." He looked at Christian. "There will be no brushback pitches. Understood?"

Begrudgingly, Christian nodded.

The umpire looked at Brooke. "And no punches. Understood?"

Brooke nodded.

The game started minutes later, and, as always, it was a pitcher's duel between Christian and Alex. Every time Christian struck out a batter, Alex did the same. Neither boy had given up a single hit when Brooke stepped up to the plate in the third inning.

Christian glared at her from behind his mask. In a way, it made him look even scarier than before, like a serial killer from an old horror movie. But unlike in prior games, he said nothing to her, not a word. His first pitch was a nasty curveball for strike one. His second pitch was a fastball that she swung at and missed. She fouled away the next two pitches, but then struck out on a wicked breaking ball in the dirt.

As she walked back to the dugout, she was mad at herself for striking out, but she was also relieved. Christian hadn't thrown a single pitch anywhere near her. Hopefully it would stay that way all day.

The game was still scoreless when she batted again in the fifth. Once again she went down swinging. She didn't want to, but she had no choice but to give Christian credit. If nothing else, he was a good pitcher. Next to Alex, he was the best pitcher she had ever seen.

The game was still scoreless in the bottom of the sixth, and Alex was throwing a gem of a game. He had only given up one hit all day, a little blooper in the second, and he was absolutely overwhelming Alderwood's batters. He had struck out ten of them so far and he was showing no signs of letting up. Since he was a senior, it was his last game as a high school player and he wanted to go out in style.

But then disaster struck. Christian, of all people, was batting and he got a hold of one of Alex's pitches and lined it straight up the middle. It was a rocket of a shot, and it hit Alex in his pitching arm, just above his elbow. He fell to the ground immediately, and he did so clutching his arm. The ball rebounded to the side. Brooke got to it quickly and threw it to first, getting Christian out, but nobody (except the umpire) even noticed.

They were all too busy looking at Alex. He was hurt. Bad. Coach West called time and rushed to the mound to help him, as did the team's athletic trainer. After a couple of minutes, Alex managed to get back to his feet, but his arm was in bad shape. He could move his fingers a little and somewhat make a fist, but that was all. He tried to raise his arm above his head, to mimic a pitch, but he could only get it part way up before the pain was too intense and he had to stop and lower it.

"It's going to need x-rays," Coach West said. "I think it's broken."

Brooke felt awful. In a way, she felt even worse than when she herself had been injured. At least when she had been injured, it had been over quickly. She had blacked out seconds after the ball had hit her. But now, just standing there, watching Coach West lead Alex back to the dugout, she felt so worthless. She wanted to help but there was nothing she could do.

Christian didn't make things any better. From Alderwood's dugout, he said, "Poor Alex has a boo-boo."

Brooke was so infuriated she was tempted to run over and punch him in the face again, but she knew she'd never get close before the umpires would catch her and throw her out. And regardless, she knew that that wasn't the best way to deal with him. If she wanted to deal with him properly, she needed to deal with him by winning the game.

But it wasn't going to be easy. They were in trouble. The game was still scoreless, but they had lost their star pitcher. And she wasn't certain they were a match for Alderwood without him.

But they had to try. Jamie took over pitching and despite getting only a couple of minutes to warm up, he did a good job. He quickly got the final two outs to finish the inning.

Brooke overheard Alex as she entered the dugout. He was sitting next to his dad discussing things with him.

"I'll go to the hospital after the game. I'm not leaving until then."

"Son," his dad said. "We need to go now. Your arm could be really damaged."

"I don't care. I worked my entire life for this game and I'm not leaving until it's over."

His dad was clearly unhappy, and he clearly didn't agree with the decision, but he said nothing more. He knew his son wasn't going to budge an inch on the issue.

As Brooke stepped into the batter's box for her next at-bat, she could tell Christian was happy. There was a twisted smile on his face, and he rocked back and forth on the balls of his feet like a little kid. He had Silver Lake right where he wanted them. Without their ace, he knew it was just a matter of time before they would falter.

And Brooke didn't help any. She went down swinging on three straight pitches. To her, Christian seemed even better than before. Now that Alex was gone, he could smell blood and he was circling in for the kill.

But then he got a surprise. Silver Lake was a great team with Alex, but even without him, they were still pretty good. Jamie was the next batter, and he refused to surrender, even for a second. He fouled off pitch after pitch after pitch after pitch. Brooke lost count after the eighth. She had never seen anything like it. No matter what Christian would throw, no matter how nasty it was, he couldn't get it past Jamie. As a result, it seemed like the duel between them would go on forever.

And then it happened. Christian got frustrated and did something he rarely did.

He made a mistake. He threw a pitch straight down the middle, and Jamie hit it a mile. Brooke knew it was a home run the second it left his bat. Everyone cheered and mobbed Jamie at home plate. Thanks to him, they finally had the lead, 1-0. Now all they had to do was hold it.

As Brooke took the field to start the bottom half of the seventh inning, she could hardly believe it. They were three outs away from the state championship. It was so close she could taste it. If everything went according to plan, they would be holding the trophy within minutes.

Unfortunately, things did not go according to plan. The first Alderwood batter hit one of Jamie's pitches into left field for a single. And then the second batter walked. And so did the third. Before Brooke could blink an eye, the bases were loaded and there was nobody out.

Coach West called time and walked quickly to the mound. He tried to hide it, but he was nervous, too. Had they come this far, just to falter in the final inning?

"Jamie. What's up?"

"I don't know, Coach." His face was flush and his eyes were wide.

Brooke didn't say anything but she knew. He was scared. He had never been in a situation like that before. He was a second baseman, but he was being asked to pitch to one of the best teams in the state in the final inning of the biggest game of the year. Anyone, even a player as good as Jamie, would crack under the pressure.

"Son," Coach West said. "You're doing just fine. You just need to calm down. With that home run you just hit, you're the hero of the game. You don't need to do much more, and you don't need to do anything fancy. Just throw strikes. Okay?"

Jamie's only response was a curt nod.

Without another word, Coach West turned and walked back to the dugout.

Brooke was really sweating now. Jamie wasn't the only one who was being affected by the pressure. It was affecting her, too. Her heart was pounding in her chest and a bead of sweat was trickling down her side, right under her jersey.

Please, Jamie, she thought. *Please throw a strike. Please. Please.*

And he did.

The only problem was the batter saw it coming and crushed it. He hit a perfect line-drive, approximately ten feet above the ground, and he hit it so hard it would have destroyed an average shortstop.

But Brooke wasn't an average shortstop. She was ready. She jumped straight up, snagged the ball out of the air for the first out, then landed and turned instantly to second. The runner on second, thinking the ball was going to get past her, had immediately left the base. By the time he realized she had gotten it and was holding it in her mitt, he was only a step away from her.

She reached out and tagged him for the second out.

Then, without even thinking, she turned to first. The runner there, too, had made a mistake and had left the base. But he had realized what had happened and had turned to dive back to safety. Unfortunately for him, he wasn't there yet.

Brooke had a brief flashback of her first day of baseball practice, her first day with the team, when she had been unable to make good, accurate throws to Blake at first, but that flashback didn't faze her for a second. With no hesitation at all, she let the ball fly, as hard as she could, and unlike her throws on that first day of practice, this one was an absolute fireball, and it was perfectly placed. It sounded like an explosion as it entered Blake's outstretched mitt.

At first, she didn't even realize what she had done. She just stood there as her teammates swarmed her. JJ got there first, then Terrell, Jamie, Skinny, Blake, and even Alex, injured arm and all.

She had won the championship by turning a game-ending triple play.

Chapter 30

The following week, there was a celebration to honor the team's accomplishment and a 'Washington State Champions' banner was hoisted into the rafters of the school's gymnasium. Everyone cheered as Alex, his arm in a cast, took the stage and made a speech on behalf of the entire team. They cheered even louder when Coach West joined him on the stage and they presented the year's 'Most Valuable Player' award to Jamie. Jamie was all smiles as he accepted the trophy, and he gave hugs to both Coach West and Alex.

But the highlight of the day for Brooke wasn't the celebration, but afterward. Alex invited them to his house, and everyone from the baseball and softball teams was there. Brooke mingled in the house for a while, then made her way to the patio. Much to her surprise, Alex was sitting by himself in a chair next to the pool. He was staring at the water and appeared to be lost in his thoughts.

She took the seat next to him. "What are you doing out here?"

"Just thinking about things."

"Like what?"

"It was such a crazy season. With you coming along, and the battles with Christian, and now the championship. I guess I just needed a couple of minutes to slow down and unwind a bit. It's funny how quickly things move these days. The whole season seems like a blur to me."

She couldn't help but agree.

He smiled at her. "What was it like?"

"What do you mean?"

"When you turned that triple play. It was incredible. Do you know how rare triple plays are? They're even rarer than no-hitters."

Brooke tried to act cool, like she'd done it a million times. "I was just doing my job, playing my position. That's what we shortstops do."

Alex raised an eyebrow. "I've been playing baseball my entire life and I've never seen a shortstop turn a triple play before."

"That's because you've been watching boy shortstops. Girl shortstops are the talented ones."

They both laughed, then turned as two people appeared at the far end of the patio, near the entrance to the kitchen. It was Jamie and Alyssa. Alyssa smiled.

The guys are right, Brooke thought. Alyssa did have a gorgeous smile. No wonder they were all so gaga about her.

"We're out of chips," Jamie said, "so we're going to run down to the store and get some more. Do you guys want anything?"

"I'm good," Alex said.

"Me, too," Brooke said.

Without another word, they turned and left. Alex watched silently as they disappeared from view.

"You okay with that?" Brooke asked.

"With what?"

"With Jamie and Alyssa. As a couple? Here?"

Alex shrugged. "I invited them. Like you said, we need to move on. It's the right thing to do."

Brooke felt bad for him, because he was clearly still heartbroken over the break-up, but at least he was handling it okay and was transitioning properly.

"I've been meaning to ask you," he continued. "And feel free to stop me if you think I'm being too forward. I'm not really ready for a serious relationship yet, but if I were, would I ever have a chance with a girl like you? I mean, I'm not a big-time two-sport softball/baseball star like you, but there are a few things about me you might like."

Brooke nearly fell into the pool. She tried to calm herself and stay as cool and as collected as possible, but it wasn't easy, not at all, since the thought of being Alex's girlfriend was so overwhelming it actually made her lightheaded.

"You might. But you'd have to treat me really well."

"Of course I'd treat you really well. Otherwise, you'd probably get mad at me and punch me in the face like you punched Christian. Trust me, I know better, and I'm not taking any chances with Boxin' Brooke."

They laughed.

"It's getting pretty chilly out here," he said. "Let's go back inside with everyone else."

He stood up, took her hand in his, and led her inside.

She had never been so happy.

A Note from the Author

Dear Readers,

I've always liked sports stories, so this book is my attempt at writing one. The story's first draft was written in December 2009 and was originally entitled *Baseball Babe*. As is always the case with my stories, it underwent many changes before it went to print. Brooke's school was originally called Mill Creek High, and her mascot was a steelhead salmon, not a shark. I thought a shark was a little more exciting, and it also pays homage to a great softball organization from Redmond, Washington called the Northwest Lady Sharks. If you ever get a chance, go and watch a Lady Sharks' game. You will not be disappointed. Brooke's select softball team was originally called the Everett Express, and I didn't change the name until my final draft. Angels just seemed like more fun. The book's most important change, however, involved Jamie. In my original outline, I made Jamie the villain in the end, but after writing a few chapters about him, I decided I liked him too much to do that. So he stayed a good guy and even ended up winning the team's MVP award at the end of the season.

Hopefully you liked the finished product. If so, please check out my other books, including *Fastpitch Fever*, *Silence in Center*, *Dog in the Dugout*, and *Missfits Fastpitch*.

Until next time,

Jody Studdard

About the Cover

The cover of this book features Amanda Tsujikawa, a junior at Juanita High School in Kirkland, Washington. Amanda is an infielder for the Woodinville Reign, a 16u select softball team from Woodinville, Washington. She also plays baseball for several teams in the Kirkland area. Like most teenage girls, Amanda likes music, movies, and cars. She has younger twin sisters named Lindsay and Emily. She is an excellent student and she'd eventually like to be an orthodontist, cancer researcher, marine biologist, or an attorney. She graduates from high school in early summer 2012.

Turn the page for a
preview of another
exciting story by
Jody Studdard

Silence
In
Center

The Tryout

Some days suck. May 15, 2013 was one of them. It started off okay but, as was sometimes the case, went downhill fast. I had a tryout with a fastpitch softball team called the Edmonds Express, which was a 14u select team from Edmonds, Washington, a small city about twenty minutes north of Seattle. I was really excited (and a bit nervous) because I had never played select softball before. I had played Little League for three years and I had made the Mill Creek All-Star team all three years I had played, but I had never tried to move up to the select level until then. The tryout was at a nice field in downtown Edmonds not too far from the city's high school. The team's coaches were friendly and outgoing, but it was still pretty intimidating, especially at first, because there were so many girls there (I'd guess around a hundred total, but there may have been more). The Express was usually a really good team, so a lot of girls from all around Seattle wanted to play for them and it was hard to win a spot unless you could really find a way to stand out and impress the coaches.

Which, at first, I thought I had done. There were six of them total, and they had us break into groups of ten girls each and go through various drills set up all over the field. My group was led by a man named James Harbaugh, who was a tall, lean man in his early forties with short, black hair, gray eyes, and a thick beard. I didn't know it at first, but later found out from some of the other girls he was the team's head coach (originally, for some unknown reason, I thought he was one of the assistants). Anyway, he led us to the infield and had us form a single-file line at second base, then hit us a series of ground balls. Each girl got five, and I fielded them cleanly and whipped them over to first as fast as I could (an assistant was covering the base for us). When we were all done with our grounders, he had us jog out to the outfield and he hit fly balls to us. At that point, I was really excited because on my Little League team I was the center fielder so fly balls were my specialty. He hit me three in a row, which I caught easily (on one of them, I didn't even have to move), so then he decided to challenge me a little by hitting one to my left. I had to run about twenty feet to get to it, but I had always been pretty fast (my dad called me a speedster) so I was able to catch it almost as easily as I caught the first three. Seeing I could catch balls on the run, he decided to really challenge me by hitting one deep into the outfield way over my head. I was forced to run all of the way to the outfield's warning track, and I ended up less than five feet away from the outfield fence itself, but I was able to make the catch anyway.

I was about as happy as I could be. Harbaugh smiled and nodded as I made the final catch, and I could tell he was impressed, at least a little. And he wasn't the only one. Sitting in the stands, watching everything intently, was my dad. He was a big sports fan and there was nothing he loved more than watching me play softball, so this was not only a big day for me but for him as well. He really wanted to see me win a spot and begin playing at the select level.

"Way to go, Melody," he called. "Well done."

From there, we moved to an adjacent field and did some hitting drills. Like always, we took turns, and Harbaugh pitched five balls to each of us. There were three girls who went before me, and they all did well. The first girl hit all five of her pitches sharply, including two that went all of the way to the warning track. The next girl fouled her first pitch away, but then made up for it by hitting the next four straight up the middle. The girl after her hit all five of her pitches into the outfield, and one of them hit and bounced off of the outfield fence. It was a great hit, and a great overall performance. But it wasn't as good as what I did. I hit my first three pitches straight up the middle, then finished by hitting the final two completely out of the park. The first cleared the fence by about five feet, and the second by about twenty. I was all smiles as I watched the second fly into the distance.

After hitting, Harbaugh got out a stopwatch and timed us running from home plate to first base. Each of us got two tries, which was good, since my first time was only so-so, but my second was really good, and I actually got the third best time of the day. After that, we called it good and wrapped things up, and I felt really confident. I felt like I had done everything possible to make the team, and I felt like I had a good chance of doing so. And I got even more excited when my dad and I were walking toward our car in the nearby parking lot and Harbaugh called out to us to wait up for a second. At the beginning of the tryout, he had told us he would not be making any roster decisions for a couple of days, since he liked to mull things over for a while, but I thought maybe he had changed his mind and had decided to offer me a spot immediately since I had done so well.

My dad seemed equally excited and I could see a definite glint of hope in his eyes as Harbaugh jogged up to us. Unfortunately, however, our excitement, and our hopes for making the team, were short lived.

"Thanks for waiting," Harbaugh said. "I wanted to thank you for trying out, and Melody, you did a great job today. Unfortunately, however, I don't think I'm going to be able to offer you a spot on the team this year."

At that, I was officially crushed. To be completely honest, I felt like my heart had been torn from my chest. I had really wanted to make the team, and since I had done so well, I thought I had.

And clearly I wasn't the only one. My dad's eyes narrowed and his face got red. He couldn't believe what he had just heard.

"Really? Why? She did great in the field and she was one of the only girls who hit an out-of-the-parker. Actually, she hit two."

Harbaugh acknowledged the comment with a smile and a nod. "Those were some nice hits. No doubt about it. Especially the second one. I knew it was gone the minute it left her bat. But anyway, my real concern isn't her skills. She's clearly got plenty of them, especially for a girl who's never played select ball before. My concern is her disability."

The minute he said the word 'disability' my dad's eyes got big. "What do you mean?"

"We've never had a player with a disability on the team before and the assistant coaches and I aren't completely confident we know how to deal with it."

At that, my dad, as had happened many times in the past when he had had to deal with similar situations, got defensive.

"She doesn't have a disability. She has a special need."

Harbaugh nodded. "Call it what you will, but I'm still not certain I'm comfortable dealing with it. I'm not certain I know how."

At this point, I should probably tell you what they were talking about. I have a severe hearing impairment, and as such I cannot hear much of anything without wearing a pair of specially designed hearing aids.

"Her Little League coaches never had any issues with it," my dad said.

"Good for them," Harbaugh said. "But Little League is a lot different than select ball. Things move quicker and are a lot more intense at the select level. I need to be able to shout commands and have my players respond to them immediately. I don't have time to do sign language."

My dad laughed. "She doesn't do sign language. With her hearing aids on, she can hear fine. Even from her spot in center field."

"Really? I didn't know that."

For a brief second, he paused, as though he was contemplating things further and reevaluating his position, and I actually thought he might have a change of heart. But much to my chagrin, his opinion didn't waiver.

"It would probably be best if she tried another team. I hear the Broncos are looking for some players. They might be willing to give her a chance."

At that, my dad (who never had much patience when dealing with people like Harbaugh) clearly had heard enough.

"Fine. Thank you for your time today, Coach." He said the word 'coach' like it was venom in his mouth. "We'll contact the Broncos. But mark my words. You're going to regret this decision one day. It's just a matter of when and where."

He said it with such conviction it actually made Harbaugh's eyes get big for a second. Not knowing what else to do, he turned and, without saying anything more, jogged back to the dugout where the other coaches were waiting for him.

My dad turned to me.   "Come on, Melody. Let's go."

I had barely gotten into the car and was still struggling to get my seatbelt on (the thing was such a beast at times), when I was flooded with emotion and started to cry. I just couldn't believe what had happened, nor how quickly things had changed.   One minute, I thought I had made the team for sure, and the next minute I was sent packing.

My dad looked over and saw the tears running down my cheeks. He was irritated, but now his irritation had shifted from Harbaugh to me.

"What are you doing?"

"What do you mean?"

"Why are you crying?"

"Why wouldn't I? I just got rejected, for the third time in a week. And for the same reason each time."

It was true. The Express tryout was the third one I had had that week, and despite doing well at each, I had been rejected each time. The minute the coaches found out I had a hearing impairment, they got nervous and didn't know what to do about it. And then they reacted exactly like Harbaugh. They tried to be nice, and they tried to do their best to not hurt my feelings or offend me in any way, but they cut me anyway. And they did it because they made the same mistake so many people made when they were dealing with me. They assumed that since I needed hearing aids, I needed a lot of other things, too, and as such I was going to be a burden. But it wasn't like that at all. I didn't need anything special, other than a chance. And they didn't have anything to worry about when it came to me personally. I wouldn't let them down. I knew I wasn't the best softball player in the world, and I probably never would be, but I always tried hard, and I always gave one hundred percent. In three years of Little League play, I had never missed any games and I only missed one practice and that was because I caught the flu the week before, which was actually quite ironic since I had just gotten my yearly flu shot.

"We'll find you a team," my dad said. "You just have to be patient."

I had heard that before. After each tryout. "I've been patient. Three times now. Let's face it, dad, it's just not going to happen. Maybe I should just stick with Little League. My Little League coaches are used to dealing with me and they accept me for what I am. Maybe select ball is a bad idea."

My dad looked at me with a disappointed look on his face. "I thought you wanted to play select ball. Originally it was your idea."

I sighed. It was true, I did want to play select ball, badly, and it had indeed been my idea. "I guess some things just weren't meant to be."

At that point, as you can probably tell, I was so disappointed and so heartbroken I was contemplating giving up softball completely. Even Little League.

But my dad would hear none of it. "What are you doing?"

"What do you mean?"

"You're making excuses. What do I always tell you about making excuses?"

I sighed. Like most dads, my dad was extremely stubborn at times and when it came to my hearing impairment he was even more stubborn than normal. Over the years, he had refused to let me use it as an excuse and he had always insisted that despite needing hearing aids, I could do anything I wanted as long as I was willing to work hard, keep my chin up, and most importantly, never give up.

As such, I had no choice but to quote his motto, which I had heard seemingly a million times over the years.

"No excuses."

"Exactly. We'll find you a team. You just have to have some faith. Eventually, we'll find a coach who will be willing to give you a chance, and then you're going to become one of the best select players in the state. Just you wait and see."

At that point, I wanted to believe him, but I was still filled with uncertainty and doubt. As such, I didn't say anything more and instead just turned and stared out the window at nothing in particular.

Without another word, my dad started the car, put it in gear, and we headed for home.

**Turn the page for a
preview of another
exciting story by
Jody Studdard**

**Kiana Cruise
Apocalypse**

Chapter 1

Amanda Anderson took a deep breath as she stepped into the batter's box. She dug her cleats into the dirt, then tapped her bat on the far side of the plate, carefully positioning herself for the next pitch. It was the bottom half of the final inning and her team, Anaheim High, was losing to their archrivals, Western High, 4-3. Luckily, however, the bases were loaded, so if Amanda could get a hit, even something as weak as a bloop single, the runner from third would score and the game would be tied. Even better, however, would be if Amanda could hit a line drive or something into a gap in the outfield, either of which would score the runner from second and Anaheim would win.

That was the good news.

Here was the bad news.

There were two outs. So if Amanda didn't get a hit, right there, right then, the game would be over and Anaheim would lose.

Most batters would be pretty nervous in a situation like that. But not Amanda. She had played softball for her entire life and it was one of her two passions (taekwondo was the other). She was one of Anaheim's best players, and as such, she lived for moments like that. She could barely contain her excitement as she waited for the pitch.

Unfortunately, however, it was nasty. Western's pitcher was a tall, blonde girl named Hailey Davidson, and she could throw several different types of pitches, all well, but her best by far was a wicked fastball. It was crazy fast. It blazed by Amanda so quickly she didn't even have time to swing at it.

"Strike one," blue called. In softball, the players called the umpires blue because they usually wore blue uniforms.

Amanda took a couple of practice swings, then got ready for the next pitch, which was another fastball, but this one was down in the dirt for ball one. The next pitch was a curve, just inside for ball two. The pitch after that was another of Hailey's nasty fastballs, but this time Amanda was able to get a piece of it and foul it away. It bounced off of the fence in front of the bleachers where the parents sat.

That was when Amanda noticed something strange. Her dad, James, was not in the bleachers. That was highly unusual since he loved softball and had always been her biggest fan. He rarely missed games (only when he was out of town on business trips), and when he was there, he was normally in the front row, cheering her on and shouting quick tips and advice to her from his seat. In a situation like that, where she had a chance to win a game, he would have been riveted to the action.

But not on that day. Instead of sitting in his normal place in the front row, he was standing to the side of the field, down the first base foul line, and he seemed to be preoccupied with two men who were sitting in the bleachers' top row. Both of them wore long overcoats and they looked European, possibly German or Russian, with sharp cheekbones and pale skin. James was watching them closely, from afar, and they seemed equally interested in him since they kept shooting quick glances his way.

Amanda had no idea what was going on since she had never seen the men before and didn't recognize them, but regardless, it wasn't something she could worry about at that point. She was down to her final strike and if she didn't do something quickly the game would be over and Anaheim would lose.

She did not want that to happen.

And it didn't.

The next pitch was another of Hailey's dreaded fastballs, and it was arguably the nastiest one she had thrown all day. It looked like a bright, yellow blur as it came at Amanda. But Amanda was not intimidated, not in the least, and she did exactly what she had been taught. She kept her chin down, her hands up, and she whipped her bat around as quickly as she could. She hit the ball perfectly and it raced toward the outfield fence. Western's center fielder chased after it and made a diving attempt to catch it, but the ball landed a foot beyond her mitt and bounced away from her.

That was all it took. Amanda's teammates and the fans in the bleachers went wild, cheering and whistling loudly as the runner who had been on second base stepped on home plate, officially winning the game. Everyone mobbed Amanda as she returned triumphantly to the dugout, and they patted her on the helmet and the back, and several of them gave her hugs.

She had done it. She had come through in the clutch and won the game. It was a total rush.

But unfortunately, her glory was short-lived. She was still celebrating with her teammates when James walked up behind her and in a stern voice said, "Amanda, we need to go. Now." He put extra emphasis on the word 'now,' and the tone of his voice was more than urgent.

Amanda was completely puzzled. This was totally out of character for him. Normally, in that type of scenario, after winning a big game, he would have been ecstatic. He would have been the one leading the team's celebration, not calling for its end. He probably would have taken them out to dinner to celebrate. But on that day, he did not look happy at all. His face was completely serious and there was obvious concern, and a little fear, in his eyes.

"What's up?" she asked.

"I don't have time to explain. Just get your stuff and let's go."

"I want to celebrate a little more with –"

"Amanda. We need to go. You're endangering everyone by staying."

She had no idea what he was talking about. Danger? At a softball game? She had never heard of anything so ridiculous.

Regardless, she knew better than to argue with him, especially at a time like that when he seemed so serious, so she rounded up her gear, placed it in her softball bag, and walked with him to his car in the adjacent parking lot. He was walking at a brisk pace, much faster than normal, and she struggled to keep up with him (James was a tall man with quite a stride). As they walked, he kept looking back at the two men who had been in the bleachers during the game. They were now behind them, also walking toward the parking lot. The minute Amanda and James got to his car he popped the trunk open, grabbed her bag from her, and tossed it inside. He slammed the trunk shut and jumped into the driver's seat as Amanda took her place next to him.

Just as she was closing her door, she noticed the two men were now at the far side of the parking lot, climbing into a car of their own, a red Audi TT. One of them was talking on a cellular phone and the other was looking directly at her. He had a nasty scowl on his face.

"What's up with those two? They're pretty creepy."

James didn't answer. Instead, he pushed two buttons on the car's dashboard right below its stereo.

"Computer," he said. "Activate voice recognition. Access code 102470."

In response, and much to Amanda's surprise, a voice came from the dash. "Voice recognition activated, agent Anderson."

Amanda was in total shock. James had had the car for a little over a year, and it was a nice car, a navy Dodge Charger, but she never knew it had voice recognition capabilities.

"Activate main monitor," James said. "Contact agent Jones. Priority one."

Amanda watched in complete amazement as the dash in front of her transformed. The dash's entire middle compartment, including the stereo and the car's heating and air conditioning controls, rotated and disappeared and was replaced by a fancy computer screen. An image of a man's face appeared on the screen the minute it appeared. The man was athletic and was in his mid to late thirties, with dark hair and deep, brown eyes.

"James," the man said. "What's up?"

"We've got a problem. And it's a big one. I'm at my daughter's game at Anaheim High. Two agents are here. Clearly foreign and clearly hostile."

"That's not possible. There's no way anyone could have discovered where you live."

"Well, someone did. As such, I need immediate assistance and extraction."

"I'm on my way."

"And Jones," James said. "Just so we're clear. Amanda is in the car with me."

Jones nodded. "I'll send everything I've got."

Without another word, his image vanished.

Amanda was starting to get worried. Her mind was on overdrive, trying to process all of the information she had seen and heard, but she was totally confused and had no idea what was going on. Why did James have all of this fancy equipment in his car, who was this man named Jones on the screen, and who were these 'foreign agents' James seemed so concerned about?

"What's going on, dad?"

"I'm not allowed to say much. Let's just say we need to get out of here right now. But don't worry. Everything will be okay."

He backed the car out of its parking spot, then drove along the street that ran in front of Amanda's school. As he drove, he kept glancing in the rearview mirror. Amanda turned and looked back and she could see the two men in the red Audi following them.

"Who are those men? Why are they following us?"

"They're a couple of associates."

"Associates? What type of associates?"

Amanda's head was really spinning now. James was a salesman at a local car dealership. Why would any of his associates at the car dealership want to follow him to his daughter's softball game? And even if they had, why would he be so concerned about them? He was acting like their lives were in danger. As such, he clearly wasn't telling her everything and it was starting to frustrate and frighten her.

"What's going on?" she demanded. "And what's up with the equipment in the car? I've never seen anything like it. I've ridden in this car a hundred times and I never knew it had equipment like this. And who is that Jones you were talking to on the screen?"

"I'll tell you later, Amanda. I need to concentrate right now."

He had pulled onto one of Anaheim's main drives, a long street heading northbound through town, and was weaving in and out of traffic, lane to lane, very quickly. Amanda had never seen him drive like that before. Normally, he was a conservative driver and he never went over the speed limit, especially when Amanda was in the car with him. But right then, he was already up to fifty miles per hour in a thirty-five mile per hour zone, and he was showing no sign of letting up on the gas anytime soon.

In the meantime, the red Audi was right behind them. And if that wasn't enough, another car, a gray BMW, had joined it.

James spoke to the screen again. "Computer. Contact agent Jones."

The man he had spoken to earlier appeared on the screen.

"Status?" James asked.

"I have several agents en route. Estimated time of arrival is less than five minutes. You?"

"Heading for I-5. I'm going to try to lose them there. In the meantime, I've got two confirmed tails and possibly two more. I'm definitely going to need some assistance. As far as I can tell, they -"

He was going to say something more when there was a loud thud. Amanda jolted forward in her seat. The car behind them, the red Audi, had moved to the side but the second car, the gray BMW, had moved forward and rammed them from behind.

"Is your belt on?" James asked, glancing over at her. His eyes were large with concern.

"Yes," she said. "Like it's always on when we're in the car, dad. But we're not normally being chased by a bunch of lunatics."

"I know. Don't worry. I've dealt with this type of situation before. I've got everything under control." He turned to the computer screen. "Computer, activate oil slick, five second spray, maximum dispersal."

"Confirmed," the computer voice responded. "Oil slick activated."

Less than a second later, a steady stream of thin, black oil sprayed from the rear of the car, covering the ground directly in front of the pursuing BMW. The car's driver saw the slick but he reacted too slowly and drove right over it. His wheels lost traction the second they touched it and he spun to the side, completely out of control. He came to an abrupt and violent stop as he smashed through a wooden fence and hit the side of a small building. Chunks of wood, metal, and glass flew in all directions.

Amanda was completely in awe. For a brief second, her fears faded away and they were replaced with curiosity.

"This car has an oil spray? That's so cool. It's just like in those old spy movies we used to watch."

"I had it installed last year," James said. "I knew it would come in handy someday."

"Sweet."

Unfortunately, she didn't get to say anything more. A third car, a yellow Porsche, darted out of nowhere and joined the chase. It hit them from behind, shaking them badly (even worse than when the BMW had hit them).

"Use the oil again," Amanda said.

"I can't. I used it all up on the first car. It's a limited supply. But don't worry. We've got other options." He turned back to the dash. "Computer. Activate smoke screen."

Less than a second later, a panel on the back of the car slid open and a thick plume of dark, gray smoke poured from within. The pursuing Porsche was totally engulfed and vanished completely for a few seconds. The driver, not being able to see even five feet in front of him, panicked, slammed on his brakes, and spun hard to the side. He ended up nose down in a nearby ditch.

But unfortunately, as fast as the smoke screen had formed, it was gone. And the original vehicle, the red Audi with the two European men inside, was back behind them, and if that wasn't bad enough, a fourth vehicle, a white Mazda RX-7, had joined it. James weaved in and out of traffic, desperately trying to avoid them, then raced onto a ramp that led up and onto Interstate 5. As soon as they got onto the freeway, he hit the gas pedal as hard as he could and they surged forward, even faster than before, maneuvering through traffic at an absolutely breakneck pace. Amanda had never gone so fast in her entire life. She watched wide-eyed as James dodged to the left to avoid a white minivan, then swerved to the right to miss a red semi truck, then veered two lanes back to the left to avoid a school bus filled with children.

But then her heart stopped.

James's Charger was fast, but the other two cars were even faster. As such, they kept up, and the Mazda moved to their right and swerved toward them, smashing into the Charger's passenger side right next to Amanda. The door panel caved in right next to her right leg, nearly crushing it. James struggled with the steering wheel and was barely able to keep them from spinning out of control, but then slammed on the brakes unexpectedly, sending the Mazda shooting forward in front of them. He let up on the brakes and sped along again.

"Brace yourself," he told Amanda as he caught back up to the Mazda. "This could get ugly. Computer, acquire target, directly ahead. Fire missile upon target lock."

Amanda's jaw dropped as a thin, gray missile flew from the Charger's grille and hit the Mazda, destroying it completely. There was a massive explosion and chunks of flaming metal, plastic, and glass rained down on them from above. Amanda's heart skipped a beat as a tire came out of nowhere and soared right over them, missing them by less than a foot.

James spoke to the screen. He was calm but there was unmistakable urgency in his voice. "Jones, I need your location. Now."

The man he called Jones appeared on the screen. "We're here. We see you. Just hold on for a few more seconds."

In the distance, just coming into view was a small helicopter, and it was racing right toward them. But unfortunately it did not arrive in time. The car behind them, the red Audi, pulled next to them, directly to their left. The passenger rolled down his window, pulled out a gun (a large pistol of some sort), and fired. The window next to James shattered, sending chunks of glass spraying all over him. Temporarily distracted and disoriented, he lost control of the car and it lurched violently to the right, hit another car that was in the lane next to it, and flipped. It rolled down the freeway, end over end, completely out of control. It turned over at least five times, maybe ten, maybe more, then came to a stop upside down in the exact middle of the freeway. It was engulfed in smoke and was a complete mangled mess of glass and metal.

The last thing Amanda heard before blacking out was the sound of James's voice next to her. He was completely desperate and frantic.

"Amanda. Are you okay? Amanda. Jones, I need an ambulance. Now."

Amanda awoke in a hospital bed, hooked to an intravenous drip and countless other tubes and wires. She had no clue what most of them were for, but the sheer number of them frightened her. She was completely disoriented and had a pounding headache that felt so bad she thought her forehead was going to explode. She was barely conscious, and she couldn't see much of anything because one of her eyes, her left one, was completely swollen shut and her other eye was blurry. She only stayed conscious for a few minutes but it was just long enough to overhear James, standing on the far side of the room talking to the man she had seen on the screen in the car. The one he had always referred to as Jones.

"That's not an option," James said. "I don't want her exposed to this type of life. I've tried to keep her out of it for years."

"We've had this discussion before," Jones said. "This is the perfect time to bring her in. You'll never get a better chance. This is an unfortunate accident, there's no doubt about that, but it's also a great opportunity."

"I don't like it, not one bit."

"There's nothing you can do. She already saw too much. What are you going to tell her? This was all just a mix-up? A freak accident? She's a smart girl, James, she'll never buy it. And you know how much the agency needs new agents, especially young ones like her. She's the perfect age for the teen program. And if she's anything like her old man, and I know she is, she'll turn out to be one of the best agents we've ever had."

James hesitated for a second. "I'm so mad I can barely think right now. I wanted my daughter to do something different. Something safe. I don't want her to end up like her mother."

"I didn't want my daughter to join the program either. But look at how she's doing. You've got to admit she was invaluable during the recent op in Cuba. Amanda will be okay, James. And I bet she'll enjoy being an agent. Just you wait and see."

James was quiet for a long while, clearly weighing his options, but then he let out a loud sigh of resignation. "If anything happens to that girl, Jones, I'm going to hold you personally responsible."

"Whatever," Jones said. "Let's get the doctor. We need to move her as soon as possible."

A few seconds later, a doctor, a nurse, and two technicians wearing scrubs entered the room and wheeled her away.

Ten minutes later, according to official documents, she died.

Glossary of Key
Softball Terms

At-bat: A player's turn to bat while her team is on offense. Players take turns batting. In a typical seven inning game, a player will usually get three or four at-bats.

Batting Order: The order in which batters take turns hitting during a game. The batting order is usually chosen by the team's coach or its manager at the beginning of the game. The batter who bats first is called the 'leadoff hitter,' and the fourth batter is called the 'cleanup hitter.' Many players see it as a promotion to be moved up in the order (closer to the leadoff batter), since they will get more at-bats per game, and they see it as a demotion to be moved down in the order.

Ball: A pitch that travels outside of the strike zone that the hitter does not swing at. If a pitcher throws four balls to a batter, before she gets three strikes, it results in a walk.

Blue: An informal term used to refer to the umpires. It originates from the traditional color of their uniforms.

Bunt: A soft hit produced by holding the bat in a stationary position over home plate. Bunts are often used strategically to advance a base runner to the next base. There are several different types of bunts, including 'sacrifice bunts' and 'push bunts.' During a sacrifice bunt, the batter intentionally tries to bunt the ball in a way so the defensive players will throw her out at first, thus allowing a base runner to advance safely to the next base. During a push bunt, a batter tries to reach first base safely by pushing the ball between the defenders just out of their reach.

Change-up: A pitch that is thrown to a batter much slower than a pitcher's other pitches. It is also called a 'change.'

Count: The term used to describe a batter's balls and strikes during her at-bat. The number of balls is listed first, followed by the number of strikes. If blue says, "The count is two and one," he's telling everyone the batter has two balls and one strike.

Curveball: A pitch that curves as it heads toward home plate.

Double play: A play in which the defense records two outs. If the same player makes both outs, with no help from any other player, it is called an 'unassisted double play.'

Error: A ruling charged to a defensive player if she makes a mistake that should have resulted in an out.

Fair ball: A ball that, when hit, lands between the two foul lines and stays in bounds past first or third base. A home run is considered a fair ball.

Fastball: A type of pitch thrown to a batter. It is usually extremely fast (thus, the name).

Fastpitch: Fastpitch is a type of softball where the pitcher is allowed to pitch the ball as hard and as fast as she wants. In slowpitch softball, the pitcher is not allowed to throw the ball hard.

Fielders: The players who are playing defense and trying to get the batters and runners out.

Fly ball: A ball that is hit high into the air and is usually caught by the defenders.

Fly out: A ball that is caught by one of the defensive players before it touches the ground. The batter is out as soon as the ball is caught.

Force out: After a batter hits the ball, she must advance to first base. The defensive players can get her out by throwing the ball to first base before she reaches it. Additionally, other base runners must advance to the next base if they are forced by a base runner behind them.

Foul ball: A ball hit outside of the two foul lines. It results in a strike. If a batter already has two strikes when she hits a foul ball, the count remains the same and the at-bat continues, because a foul cannot result in a strikeout. A 'foul tip' is a type of foul ball that is hit directly behind the batter.

Ground ball: A ball hit on the ground in the infield.

Ground-rule double: A hit that lands in fair territory and bounces over the outfield fence. The batter is awarded second base, and all of the runners who were on base at the time advance two bases.

Hit: A batted ball that allows the batter to safely reach base. There are several types of hits. A single is a hit that allows a batter to advance to first base. A double is a hit that allows the batter to advance to second. A triple is a hit that allows a batter to advance to third base, and a home run is a hit that allows the batter to advance all the way to home plate.

Hit and run: A play where the base runner advances to the next base as soon as the pitcher releases the ball. Usually, the batter attempts to hit the ball regardless of whether it is a ball or a strike.

Home run: A hit that allows the batter to reach home plate safely. There are several types of home runs. An out-of-the-park home run is a hit that flies over the outfield fence between the two foul poles. The batter and any runners that are on base at the time are awarded home plate and each of them scores a run. An inside-the-park home run is a hit that does not fly over the outfield fence, but the batter reaches home plate anyway. A solo home run is a home run that occurs when there are no base runners on base, and a grand slam is a home run that occurs when there is a base runner on first, second, and third bases. In Seattle, a grand slam is called a 'Grand Salami' — a term coined by the legendary sportscaster Dave Niehaus.

Inning: The individual segments of a game. Each game has seven innings. Each team gets to bat once during each inning, and it gets to continue batting, and scoring runs, until the other team makes three outs. The visiting team bats first, in what is called the 'top' of the inning, and the home team bats second, in the 'bottom' of the inning.

Line drive: A ball that is hit very hard and with a trajectory almost parallel to the ground. Players are taught to hit line drives, because it is often very difficult for the defensive players to catch them.

No-hitter: A game in which the pitcher does not allow the opposing team to get any hits. No-hitters are extremely rare, and they are seldom done by any player at any level.

Out: The defense must create three 'outs' before an inning is over.

Power hitter: A batter who is known for hitting the ball extremely hard.

Riseball: A type of pitch that starts low, like a fastball, but rises dramatically as it heads toward home plate. Many batters (including Fastpitch Fever's star, Rachel Adams) are fooled by riseballs and they swing too low and miss them.

Robbed: A term used by players to describe a play in which they lose a hit, usually because a defensive player makes an outstanding play. In Fastpitch Fever, Rachel Adams was robbed of a hit in the state's championship game when the opposing center fielder dove and caught the ball. The girl who inspired *Fastpitch Fever*, Molly McCall, was robbed on a daily basis.

Run: A run is scored when a base runner safely reaches home plate.

Sacrifice: A play where a batter intentionally hits the ball into an out situation so she can advance or score a runner.

Safe: A ruling made by blue when a base runner safely reaches a base.

Screwball: A pitch that curves toward the side of the plate from which it was thrown.

Slapper: A left-handed batter known primarily for using her speed to get to first base.

Stolen base: A play in which a runner advances safely to the next base as soon as the pitcher releases the pitch.

Strike: A pitch that a batter swings at and misses, hits foul, or fails to swing at that crosses the strike zone. A batter is out after receiving three strikes.

Strike out: A play when a batter accumulates three strikes, at which point her at-bat ends and she is out.

Strike zone: The area above home plate between a batter's knees and armpits.

Tag out: A play in which a fielder with the ball tags a base runner who is not standing on a base.

Tag up: A base runner cannot leave a base until a batted ball hits the ground. If she does, and if the ball is caught, she must return to her base. If she waits until the ball is caught, then leaves the base, the play is called a 'tag up' and she is allowed to go.

The Cycle: A term used by players to describe the 'holy grail' of softball. A player hits for the cycle when she hits a single, double, triple, and home run in the same game. It is extremely hard to do and rarely done by any player at any level. The girl who inspired Fastpitch Fever, Molly McCall, hit for a 'super cycle' during one of her Little League games: she hit a single, double, triple, home run, and she was intentionally walked by the opposing pitcher.

Triple play: A play in which the defense records three outs. If the same player makes all three outs, with no help from any other players, it is called an 'unassisted triple play.' Triple plays are extremely rare.

Walk: Four balls from a pitcher results in the batter receiving a 'walk,' and the batter automatically advances to first base. A walk is also referred to as a 'base on balls.' An 'intentional walk' is a type of walk where the pitcher intentionally throws four balls, and she does not even try to get the batter out. Intentional walks are done to avoid pitching to really good batters in key situations.

About the Author

Jody Studdard is the author of several children's novels, including *Kiana Cruise: Apocalypse*, *Fastpitch Fever*, *Escape from Dinosaur Planet*, and *The Sheriff of Sundown City*. He is a graduate of Monroe High School (1989), the University of Washington (1993), and California Western School of Law (1995). In addition to writing, he is a practicing attorney with an office in Everett, Washington. He is a fan of the Seahawks, Storm, and Sounders FC.

Visit Jody at:

www.jstuddard.com

E-mail Jody at:

jodystuddard@jodystuddard.com

Website

For more information about this book, including photos, word searches, word scrambles, discussion questions, newspaper articles, and other fun stuff, visit:

www.jstuddard.com

Made in the USA
San Bernardino, CA
20 October 2017